Wakefield Press

Street Furniture

Matt Howard lives in Sydney.
Street Furniture is his first novel.

T0359556

Street Furniture

MATT HOWARD

Wakefield
Press

Wakefield Press
1 The Parade West
Kent Town
South Australia 5067
www.wakefieldpress.com.au

First published 2004

Cover designed by Liz Nicholson, designBITE
Text designed by Clinton Ellicott, Wakefield Press
Typeset by Ryan Paine, Wakefield Press
Printed and bound by Hyde Park Press

National Library of Australia
Cataloguing-in-publication entry

Howard, Matt, 1963–   .
Street furniture.

ISBN 1 86254 646 0.

I. Title.

A823.4

Publication of this book was assisted by the
Commonwealth Government through the
Australia Council, its arts funding and advisory body.

for
Kate Farrar
Matt Wakeham
Ana Kingi
&
Maya Donevska

1.

I turned eight during the month my father left Diane and me. It took another month to be sure he had really gone because he didn't actually live with us. As the days and weeks came and went without the familiar explosions of Dave's big blue car landing outside our house my mother slowly accepted that it might just be the two of us.

Diane had the celebration of my birthday on the move that year, telling me more than once that I had the dates confused. She maintained a hope that Dave might return, like a bird that appears each spring, and she could enjoy my day better. I allowed her to think that I was young enough not to know about dates and just wondered if I might turn nine before I turned eight.

My mother probably knew that Dave was not forever but like me had hoped that now would last beyond today. I wondered where he was and selfishly wanted to think that he regretted leaving me more than my mother. Diane, who spent a lot of her new spare time watching daytime soap operas, told me not to blame myself. This hadn't occurred to me as I presumed it was understood that he had left her. Either she deserved it or Dave was not as dependable as I'd thought. I kept this to myself and while I secretly did blame her, Diane was cheered by my declaring that it must be all Dave's fault as he was the one who had done the leaving. We spent these weeks watching TV, re-reading (me the few books that the local library would never again see and my mother the dated magazines that the medical centre would never miss), and occasionally fetching kebabs from Habib's, where my mother endeared herself to all the Habibs by bringing her own cucumber for them to dice and put on our bulging beef yeeros.

Previously I hadn't given much thought to how much Dave did around the place. He controlled the TV, ordered and collected pizzas, and tended the dope plants on our small balcony that faced the third-floor balconies on the other side of our street. More importantly he kept Diane's small, unregistered car functioning – and whenever Dave came by some money so did the unhappy people at the real estate office.

Soon enough my mother was ready to be without me during the day and for me to go back to school. Our first day back amongst it started early as our modest home gave in quickly to the promise of a scorching summer's day. By seven-thirty the unit was already cooking us as though we were a pair of huge turkeys that needed to be in the oven before breakfast to make sure they were done for lunch. Diane's car started, so we drove the short distance to my school, switching the air-conditioning off as we approached the one hill the car needed to conquer.

Trying to keep the car alive my mother hugged me tightly but quickly before I leapt from the front seat to wait by the gates for the arrival of any other early-birds. As she drove off to spend the day with her friends, sitting and gossiping in the cool comfort of the Sporting Club or baking herself at the council pool, I sat down in the gutter, leaning against a marooned builder's mini-skip that offered a slash of shade.

The ground slowly guzzled the cool provided by the skip and, though usually competent with the calendar, I re-checked the digital watch Dave had left behind and which I'd taken to be my birthday present. Surely it wasn't Saturday? I spun the loose band so I could look at its face – which seemed sure it was Friday, 9:19 am. Looking around on the off chance hundreds of schoolmates had slipped past me silently and through the gates I saw nothing. No one.

I shifted myself to the bus shelter opposite the school and – without a bus-pass, money or a recent sighting of anything that resembled a bus – made myself comfortable. Each time I peered past the side-wall of the shelter, down the main road, it was not for a bus that I yearned but a big blue car that contained happy days. And though I knew he wouldn't appear, each time I looked and Dave was not there I made a promise to myself that I was through with checking. At 9:37 I decided to keep my promise. To safeguard my resolve I lay down along the bench in the shelter, my cap pulled over my eyes, and tried to think of nothing.

I was woken by two sets of eyes looking down at me. It took a while to recognise the lower set as belonging to Alex Smith – 'Smithy' – one of my classmates. With him, I guessed, was his mother. Older than Diane, she was tall and skinny like Smithy and wore a brightly coloured sun-dress to mis-match her brightly coloured lips and eye-lids. As I sat up Smithy explained to Mrs Smithy that my name was Dec and I hadn't been to school for a while so mustn't have known about the day off on account of a strike in support of people in a place he called Afghan land.

Mrs Smithy asked me if my mother or father were at home or at work and seemed to understand my confused response almost immediately. She told me her name was Bev and I could call her that if I liked. They were on their way to the shops near the railway station and I could go with them if I didn't have a key to my home.

It was then I noticed the car they had pulled up in.

It made Dave's escape machine look like a matchbox car. Bigger than a wizard's sleeve, it looked longer than some of the local streets. It didn't seem new, but its white duco gleamed at me nevertheless. A silver boomerang sat atop the bonnet.

Bev, seeing my startled face, told me that the car was given to her in place of what she was owed when the prestige limo-hire company she worked for had closed.

Smithy and I jumped into the car's vast interior, sitting opposite each other on the white padded seats that ran along the insides.

As Smithy's mother prepared to take off she turned to look at me and said firmly, 'Dec, do up your seat-belt.' She waited as I grappled with the buckle, finally giving in and clambering into the cabin and doing the belt up even tighter than Diane's drop-off hug of this morning.

Fastened securely to the wall of the limo I confidently made the first bend.

2.

My brother, Smithy, 29 like me except a few months older, arrives last. Sitting himself next to Jeff he grins broadly, sniffs the air in mock disgust, and opens today's proceedings. 'And what the fuck have you marinated yourself in?'

Maya defends Jeff in a flash. 'It's called cologne, you might try it yourself one day.'

One hand resting on her no-longer flat stomach, she grabs a chunk of ice from her Coke and throws it across the table at Smithy.

Jeff, appreciating the support, shoots her a quick smile. He adds his own feeble retaliation – 'Yeah, piss off Smithy' – then, good natured that he is, also throws Smithy a smile, though it's no match for the one he gave Maya.

Smithy starts working on his indignant act but decides just to tickle his little mate, who surrenders in giggles, his dark eyes laughing loudly.

If Smithy is our leader, the big fish in our little pond, then Jeff is our mascot. Of average height with shoulder-length, straight dark hair, parted in the centre and held behind his ears, and light skin (more from a lack of outdoor activity than melanin), his most outstanding feature are the long eyelashes that annoy him by scraping the inside of his sunnies whenever he does venture outside during the day.

Smithy looks over at Stan, behind the bar, and signals our order across the pub. Three fingers. Stan, real name unknown, and so-called because he came from one of the 'stan' countries, possibly Uzbekistan, knows that the type of drink never changes – just the quantity, depending on how many of us are assembled at the time, less Maya for now. As Stan pulls the schooners of VB, Smithy saunters across the pub's richly coloured shag pile. Tall and lean, with short-cropped mid-brown hair, rounded square face and clear light-blue eyes atop strong cheekbones, Smithy has a natural edge that many around these parts try unsuccessfully to emulate at the tattoo parlours or by putting rings through their faces. Smithy wears no adornments – not even a watch, never sunnies or caps, rarely shoes – just a look of calm defiance. Fortunately for Smithy even blemishes keep their distance.

Today being a second Thursday, we are all flush and in a few hours will be celebrating at The Golden Food Star – reducing our host's margin on his lunch-time all-you-can-eat buffet. For now, Jeff is spending some of his not-so-hard-earned at the cigarette machine, returning with the wrong brand after punching 1 then 7 when he wanted product 17. Maya, slumped in her seat, is onto her second schooner of full-strength Coke. While her pregnancy was initially a shock for all of us, including her, the savings she is making on cigarettes, alcohol and dope would make a squirrel preparing for winter blush. And though it's taken a while for the news to bring joy to Maya, the rest of us immediately realised the benefits of a perpetually straight friend who could drive the rest of us around for the best part of a year.

'Fancy a VB, Dec?' says Smithy.

Knowing this game, I still can't help playing along. 'Uh-huh.'

'Cool, me too.'

Not commanding the presence of Smithy I don't attempt to signal my order across the now bustling pub. As I head toward Stan, who is cleaning glasses with a dirty cloth, I catch Murat – 'Rat-Boy' – joining Smithy, Jeff and Maya so I order four VBs and another Coke. Stan, not much older than our gang, pulls the beers while chatting to the young blonde barmaid who for a while had had a thing going with Smithy.

I return to our table to hear Jeff suggesting that there should be two weekends each week. Now this is where you might expect Smithy to pounce. *'What difference would that make – you don't have a fucking job!'*

But Smithy holds back, as I knew he would. The

arrival of Rat-Boy, mate that he is, represents a change in dynamic to our core group of four. A certain loyalty, a type of code that he sticks to like glue, prevents Smithy taking easy shots at Jeff in front of anyone other than Maya or me.

I put the drinks on the table, and ditch the tray on the floor. 'I reckon Stan and that new barmaid might be an item in the making.'

'Onya Sherlock,' Smithy retaliates.

I like it when Smithy uses this nickname my father had given me. He knows it, too.

Maya steals a look at Smithy and tries her luck with a shot. 'Wasn't she your bit of fluff?'

'Yeah, for about five minutes.'

Maya and I look at each other trying to force the other to laugh first. Smithy beats us to it by laughing at himself then, looking directly at Maya, he continues. 'If she wasn't chewing gum, she was yapping – her fucking jaw never got a break.'

End of conversation. If it wasn't for Maya, Smithy would have entertained us with his well-worn line that for him the bar blonde had been as wet as an otter's pockets.

The Oasis Hotel is not pretty but serves its clientele what they want. The main bar sits between the TAB, which is full of Vietnamese (mostly), and on the other side The Oasis Café, which serves kebabs to the (mostly) Lebanese population of this part of

Bankstown. Here in the middle the rest of us mostly drink, smoke and play pool (between bets and kebabs). The walls of the main bar were painted, a long time ago, the muted olive colour that you see inside the precinct headquarter settings of all those 'gritty' New York cop shows. The thick carpet would disturb anyone's sense of sight and smell, I'd bet taste wouldn't fare well either if put to the test. A jukebox relaxes by the cigarette machine, Marlboros winning out over Powderfinger or Pearl Jam when money is short.

Here we sit and laugh at anyone who aims higher, or aims at all.

'What's the time, Rat-Boy?' Smithy inquires, making use of the only person among us with a watch.

'Twenty minutes until Buffet the Hunger Slayer opens,' Rat-Boy responds, assuming correctly the nature of Smithy's rare interest in time.

Smithy inexplicably assumes a high-class English accent. 'I trust you'll be joining us for the halal selection, my friend?' Smithy is generally good at whatever he attempts and his best impersonations are of the sort of folk who appear on *Jerry Springer*.

'And the Chinese, Vietnamese and Australian stuff – I'm getting my whole $14.80's worth!' Rat-Boy says.

'Well, being multicultural myself I plan to match you and raise you an Indian selection,' Smithy declares.

Rat-Boy scoffs. '*You* – multicultural – you're joking right?'

'Too right mate – my ancestors are from Ireland, Scotland, England – the whole United fucking Kingdom.'

Smithy grins across at me as I sit coasting like a pilot fish attached to a shark, dragged along for the ride with little effort.

'What's a bronco?' Jeff asks out of the blue.

'A type of wild horse,' Smithy answers automatically without even turning to Jeff, who sits next to him.

None of us now think them strange, these questions Jeff fires at any time, reminding us either that we bored him or he's just somewhere else. As a rule, Smithy handles the Science and Nature category.

'Pool, Dec,' Smithy orders, 'time for a game before eleven-thirty.'

I break, as Smithy beat me again last night in our final game before the pub closed and the core four stumbled around the corner to the large yellow block that contained the flat Smithy, Jeff and I had shared for more than five years. Maya wound up sleeping on the couch, displacing Jeff to the floor, too exhausted, despite all the Cokes she'd supped, to walk the extra distance to the place she shared with her older sister.

As we shoot in silence I watch Smithy stalking the table, and think how we all revere him, unconsciously playing this game by his rules, within his parameters. I don't baulk at this, in fact I'm glad of it – he sets a way of being and leads from the front.

Our game is slow, Smithy taking longer than usual to flog me, so the others leave ahead of us to walk the few doors to our fortnightly treat, enjoying a quick shot of sunshine as entree. By the time Smithy and I arrive Maya and Rat-Boy are hoeing into their first plate load and Jeff, an easily distracted eater as well as a notoriously slow hunter, has just returned from the food station after getting his head caught under one of the bain-marie hoods. Smithy sidles past, nods at our table of friends and greets them with 'Hi, Freaks'.

Every fortnight we plan to pace ourselves so we'll still be eating as the staff turn off the warmer switches on the slick silver food stations. Each of these six stations features luminescent pink neon lettering: 'Vietnam', 'China', 'India', 'Lebanon', 'The Sea' and 'Australia' (a mix of whatever doesn't fit into the other collections).

Maya always follows a station by station rule – setting herself a target of six plates worth of food. Starting with Asia (in no particular order), she then does the sea and wraps up with Lebanon and Australia. The rest of us buzz around the stations collecting nectar from whichever trays catch our senses.

Maya studies Rat-Boy's plate as he finishes off his first serving. 'How's the fish?' she asks.

Rat-Boy looks down at his empty plate. 'Huh? I thought it was chicken.'

3.

'Entertaining are we?' The butcher smiles as he collects the half-dozen raw chicken wings Smithy always orders for his old cattle dog Sylvia.

'Fuck off, Porky.'

The cheerful Turkish butcher laughs as he gives Smithy change from three dollars and we leave between the long, coloured strips of plastic that hang in our way. I look back through the display window of the shop to the picture of a lush field with smiling sheep and cows grazing in it. Perhaps the butcher thinks the sight of these blissful beasts in their natural state will make passers-by water at the mouth for a slab of animal flesh. Ahmed is still chuckling as he straightens the pieces of fake green grass that offer relief among the slaughter.

It's late afternoon as we head through the shopping strip that runs alongside the railway line. We're on our way to call in on Smithy's parents just in time for Friday night fish and chips. Following the path we used to take on our way home from school –

during spring we'd wear bright plastic ice-cream containers to guard against the swooping magpies – we pass through streets mostly named after trees that never grew here, those that did having been torn out since the days of maggies and ice-cream container hats. I glance to check that we are turning into Elm Street and not the disarmingly similar Oak Street or Pine Street that run parallel either side.

Smithy smokes most of the way, swinging the plastic bag of wings down the centre of the quiet streets and saying nothing. I follow him as I always have, avoiding the thoughts of insubordination that strike intermittently. Thoughts of walking ahead of my best mate, my brother. Perhaps even running ahead. Would he let me run, would he follow, would I lose him?

The older residents of Elm Street are settling into the shade of early evening, those originally from elsewhere taking their positions on the mismatched furniture that crowd their front verandahs while ageing Skips claim their backyards again to welcome the night. Across from the house that took me in more than twenty years ago the same woman who would wave from between her front curtains every time someone entered or left any house in her view waves at us now. Despite her cheery disposition we named her 'Mrs Kravitz' and, later simply 'Lenny's mother'.

We jump the low brick wall that separates Smithy

territory from the street, Smithy nearly landing on Twix, the male half of a set of twin cats both with a balance problem. Being unable to negotiate steps, Twix and his sister Twirl keep mostly to the front yard. The twins' fear of leaping means the rotting carcass of a Camira that lies abandoned in front of the garage door is forever saved the ignominy of paw prints.

Despite all this, Twix is in fact a cat ready to take on the outside world. He will happily follow at heel like a dog so long as stairs are not involved. Completely black and a little bashed-around looking from scrapes with the nearly identical Twirl, Twix has considered himself a cat above the rest ever since Sylvia was no longer a teenager and gave up leaving the house.

I step over Twirl, asleep at the base of the cement steps that climb into Smithy's house, a small insect hanging onto the tip of one of her whiskers like a pole-vaulter refusing to release.

Smithy greets his father who is in the front room channel surfing. 'Hey, Frank.'

'Hi boys,' Mr Smithy says before telling the overly peppy weatherman to fuck off.

We continue through the small house to the kitchen, where Mrs Smithy is stuffing junk mail into reply-paid envelopes that have been sent by other junk mail companies flogging insurance, credit cards and other once-in-a-lifetime crap. She gives us both a kiss and asks us to drop the bulging envelopes into the postbox when we go to pick up the fish and chips.

Traditionally on Friday nights we collect both the fish and chips order and Smithy's grandmother Maisie. She lives at the end of the street and is okay to walk up the soft incline with me and Smithy either side.

Smithy tears apart the plastic bag of wings for Sylvia, who lies at his mother's feet, and puts the open bag on the kitchen floor beside the old dog's panting smile.

I venture back to the front room to sit and enjoy the fun of listening to Mr Smithy tell the presenters and hosts that hold sway between five and seven to fuck off or get stuffed. Entering the sunlit room I hear Mr Smithy, having just been welcomed to somebody's programme, respond by welcoming the leering host to 'my fucking living room'.

When we were young, after the sun had gone down, Smithy's dad would insist that we could only have the lights on if we were going to read, otherwise the only light came from the television. Though the real reason for this was to save on the electricity bill, Mr Smithy would claim that it was good for our eyes. I spent those years reading all I could so that we didn't have to sit in the dark. Fucked if I know if it was worth it.

I sit down on the recently purchased second-hand

sofa, prompting Mr Smithy to tell me in a bemused tone that, after we'd helped him haul the old sofa down to the footpath last week, it had disappeared in five minutes, grabbed by the neighbours two doors down who shortly thereafter dumped their old lounge onto the roadside. All this recycling had been observed with much waving from Lenny's mother.

While Mr Smithy wields the remote, seeking out ad-breaks rather than shows during the lean hours that from mid-spring are no longer afternoon but not yet night, I ask him about this week's batch of videos, pointing at the empty boxes piled up under the front window.

'Any of that lot any good?'

'*The Dish* was the pick of 'em – had the caravan park owner and the surfer guy from *Sea Change*, that Kiwi actor from the Jurassic Park movies and Elaine's boyfriend from *Seinfeld* – you know, the American guy from the M&M ads. Loads of big names.'

Cricket is back on so the channel-switching stops for a while. As the remote commands a television that is only able to provide a picture, the sound having died a while back, Mr Smithy gestures for me to get up and turn down the volume provided by the ancient tubeless TV that sits beneath the silent television. He only ever bothers to synchronise picture and sound when he is confident of sticking to a programme for a while, though the exercise involved in getting up to change the station on the sound box probably does Mr Smithy no harm. With cricket and tennis no sound at all is the choice of this armchair critic but the long summers of switching between the two sports on the viewing box means that numbers 7 and 9 on the remote's soft key pads have been all but erased.

Mr Smithy asks after Maya. 'What's that nice Serbian girl up to? The one who came over that Boxing Day?'

I respond, my eyes stuck on the upper screen. 'Okay. Pregnant.'

Mr Smithy doesn't bother remembering names – you're either mate or the person who did that or drives this or came by at a certain time. Jeff is 'your little mate', Maya will be forever the Serbian girl who came over on that Boxing Day, and Rat-Boy was stuck with being the guy in the red car that dropped off the Serbian girl who came over on that Boxing Day.

Smithy and his mother join us, Smithy slumping into the empty end of the sofa and Mrs Smithy, assuming her husband and I have been sitting in total silence the whole time, muses aloud how two females sitting in silence would reckon they must be fighting with each other but two males can sit for hours, not saying a word, without a hint of a problem. After checking that her husband is ready for tea, Mrs Smithy dials ahead so that the food will be ready by the time Smithy and I get to the shop: five pieces of fish (including one for the dog), four dim-sims, a hamburger with onion and egg only – no salad (for Maisie), one fish stick, two Chiko rolls and five dollars worth of well-cooked chips.

We wave to Maisie, waiting in her doorway, as we pass her place to collect the dinner, Twix following on our heels. Smithy once told Stan the barman that in their thirties people who live on the North Shore buy their second place, while Westies of similar age organise syndicates for multi-week lotto. But whether you are in the money or not, any remaining grandparents tend to die.

As we go by the Taj Mahal Curry House and slip into the fish and chip shop I guess that Maisie may not last another full decade but hope that there are still at least a few hundred more hamburgers with onion and egg, no salad, to come.

4.

The ageing limo manoeuvred Canterbury Road while I thought about the day nearly one year earlier when I first met this long white car and its family that I had now joined. The Friday that eased into a weekend that stretched to now.

Smithy, now seemingly un-jealous of my hijacking his family, did in the early days taunt me with tales of my mother dropping me off by the side of the road and his mother collecting me like a street person finding something of mild interest while rifling through a garbage bin. Mrs Smithy, however, has always liked to tell her friends, when I am about, that picking me up was like discovering a valuable gem, mistakenly left for just a minute. She reckons she's near as stolen me.

In those first few weeks, willing Diane to leave me in my new home, I came to realise that it was me controlling this – that I'd chosen to switch over like someone jumping off of one tram as it slowed down and climbed on another passing by that was headed more directly to his destination. There'd be no getting me off of this one.

As she left a note under my mother's door that day, explaining where I was and giving her phone number for Diane to call, it's likely that Mrs Smithy knew I'd already decided how this was going to go. To make it easier on my mother there was never any collecting of my things or formal agreements. I simply shifted like a pet dog that one day moves his allegiances to a neighbour's house, leaving his bowl and part of his heart behind. The phone calls became less frequent but were always full of love – my mother had promised no more but had never offered less.

Mr Smithy turned the limo into Flathead Road as Bev dozed beside him and Maisie, Sylvia, Smithy and I tried in vain to fill the rest of the car. I was to discover that every summer one day was allocated to be spent here in Hurstville, in Great-Aunt Gaye's huge backyard, her husband Lester behind the barbecue turning sausages into charcoal in shifts throughout the afternoon as around him family, neighbours and friends played cricket or cooled down under the sprinkler.

The old weatherboard house owned the corner of Flathead Road and Snapper Street. As Mr Smithy negotiated a space large enough to land the limo Smithy and I escaped the car with puppy Sylvia at our heels, and tore through the empty house to join the folk gathered out the back.

A massive willow tree in the centre of the yard was a leading participant in the activities. Its prime job was to serve as stumps for a cricket game that had no end, though the sides and participants ebbed and flowed throughout the day. The other stumps were less distinguished – a spaceship-silver aluminium garbage can without a lid, placed midway between the willow and the near-collapsed back fence. The bin acted in its original capacity, collecting a growing pile of paper-plates, soft drink bottles and beer cans, as well as marking the bowling end of the wicket. Down the pitch the willow had a rope tied around its belly, garbage can height, to mark the top of the stumps.

As Smithy and I blended into the game, an older boy shouted the Snapper Street rules. 'You can't get out first ball, over the fence is six and out, if you reach fifty you're gone.'

The batting order was never clear, but older players made sure that everyone had their fair share by giving younger players lenient decisions in run-out calls, and hitting easy catches when they felt they'd been in too long.

Above the rope, among the branches, hundreds of hard-to-spot cicadas drummed the day's theme, the only jarring notes coming when a bird feasting on the smorgasbord of fruit trees decided to discard vegetarianism and pluck a Greengrocer, Brown Baker or a rare Black Prince out of the willow, carrying the stray note into the sky before consuming it whole.

Uncle Les had set up the barbecue in the shade of a plum tree at the back of the sprawling yard. The bulk of the food came, in fact, from inside the cool house – salads, cold chicken and ham platters – but Les was acclaimed as the chef for the day.

Once our hunger was too loud to ignore, Maisie convinced Smithy and me to abandon the cricket. We joined the older people who had stationed themselves for the day around the food table, Maisie warning us to eat our lunch before it got hot. With the sun shining we wolfed down our loaded plates as Aunty Gaye explained to the oldies, with their soft shoes and pale soft downy faces, that in fact she grew the fruit trees *so* birds would visit.

Les fed Sylvia with sausages that fell off the hot-plate while Maisie topped up the dog bowl under the backyard tap. Even though Maisie lived up the street from us it was really for her benefit that Mrs Smithy had allowed Smithy to get a puppy. Maisie's own dog – a small silky terrier called Silk – had died a few months back after a long illness. Before he died she'd seen the council workers pouring new cement paths along our street so Maisie had prepared her companion for his last walk. As the council truck turned from Elm Street, Silk was trotting across the fresh path. With this memorial of her dog alive, his footsteps recorded for eternity outside her door, Maisie was happy to scatter Silk's ashes to the wind. Every day when Maisie walked down to our house to help with the new puppy, she'd stop along the footpath to ponder Silk's paw-prints.

The sun slipped behind the fruit trees and the few women who were still smoking and gossiping while seated under the sprinkler, somehow keeping their cigarettes alight, withdrew for dryer climes. The cricket, aided by a floodlight attached to a lower branch of the magnificent willow rolled into its night-time session. The barbecue was kept on a low heat ready for a fresh round of sausages.

5.

Five years of sleeping on the couch hasn't diminished Jeff's morning disposition which, like his mood at any other given time, is content and cheerful. As I try to co-ordinate wiping the sleep out of my reddened-green eyes, flattening my short dark hair, which overnight had taught itself to stand on end, and manoeuvering myself around the debris of the previous night, Jeff is merrily already unmaking his bed by flinging his pillow and doona back on top of the fridge. The couch is now ready to perform its daytime duties. I plant myself there, my feet on the overturned recycling tub that serves as a coffee table.

Our flat is unremarkable – two small bedrooms either side of a bathroom that has no bath but does have a washing machine, a combined lounge/third bedroom and a kitchen that is home to an extended family of mice. We use the balcony that clings to the side of the flat to dry clothes fortunate enough to get a spin in the washing machine, and, like at my mother's old place, to grow a few dope plants.

I remember more than once unconsciously wiping my feet as I left our place – like Smithy I never bother when entering.

With three dole cheques each fortnight the rent is not a problem and so we stay: Smithy, our chairman of the bored, sleeping a large part of each day away; Jeff sleeping each night where he has sat most of the day; and me becoming sure that I'm losing grip on the line between asleep and awake.

Most days we rarely leave the flat while the sun is at work, especially during winter, though our feastings every second Thursday at The Golden Food Star take place whatever the season. From October our Friday visits home for fish and chips also require pre-dark outdoor activity due to daylight saving. The only other exception to our vampire-like routine comes when Maya corrals us into leaving our world for a day at the beach, causing our faces to tingle with the rare pleasure of sunshine on skin, our light tans dissipating when neglect returns once again.

Jeff joins me on the once-cream couch that faces the television and starts to pack the bong. We usually share a crammed cone or two before Smithy surfaces at the crack of noon, then the three of us drift through the remains of the day smoking, drinking and occasionally eating, if any of us can be bothered venturing to Habib's or Maccas.

Jeff passes me the bong and, keeping the cone lit,

I suck in the sweet smoke till my lungs are full. As breakfast a couple of cones can't be beat, though they hasten your appetite for a more substantial lunch.

'*Trainspotting* or *The Simpsons*?' Jeff asks, juggling an overnight hire that we've never returned, requiring us to change video stores, and one of his many home-made collections of *Simpsons*' episodes. While loading the compilation tape Jeff asks me if I think a degree is necessary to get a good job – if you wanted one, that is.

Smithy has slipped up behind us, still half-asleep and on his way to the kitchen to grab a VB. 'Oh, yeah. A degree will result in a better job – like say a dentist or accountant. Such interesting work!'

He returns with three cans and elaborates. 'If you want to spend your time with your hand in someone's mouth or tapping away on a calculator then go and spend five years at uni with a bunch of wankers from the North Shore. Not me, mate.'

That's good enough for Jeff, who accepts most of what Smithy says without question. Jeff's nature allows him to see Smithy's outburst as Smithy's way of relieving him of any misplaced notion of being a loser. Smithy is Jeff's hero – plain and simple – and the pride that Jeff takes from the fact that Smithy hangs out with him – chastising and directing him – cannot be over-estimated.

'I've applied for a job,' Jeff finally announces, his face looking to Smithy and me for reassurance.

'What doing?' I say, filling the anticipated silence.

'My father's organised for a friend of his to interview me about a job at one of those fruit stalls in the city.'

Jeff's family consists of his parents, who moved from Bankstown to an outdoor furniture franchise on the Gold Coast a few months back, two elder sisters who both now lived in Bris-Vegas, and a selection of old aunts – including an ancient blue-haired one who Jeff moans about after family weddings where she nudges Jeff in front of Maya and proclaims, 'You're next!'

'When's this interview?' I ask as Smithy gathers his thoughts.

'Two weeks.' Jeff waits nervously for the verdict, looking now just at Smithy.

Smithy snaps his fingers, points at himself then me, smiles and adopts a Cockney accent: 'We're going to have to teach you the names of some pretty exotic fruits, Jeffrey, if you're gonna serve all those posh wankers who work in the city.'

Across Jeff's face stretches a grin that extends beyond his ears. I'm pleased for Jeff, but can't help thinking about me – will I be the last one standing – or in our case lying – on the sofa? Not likely, I figure, not with Smithy resolute in his opposition to altering our days.

Smithy winks at me and, before it gets too mushy, sends Jeff off to Habib's to get some kebabs.

I picture Jeff bounding the few blocks to Habib's Yeeros and Charcoal Chicken Shop, moving quickly through the sunshine and being welcomed by one of the Habibs – middle-aged Turkish guys who all look uncannily like Saddam Hussein and call everybody 'champion'. Jeff, like my mother had done, always receives the healthiest of portions from whichever Habib is on carving duty, his relaxed even-tempered-ness a winner with the local merchants as with his mates. And always he leaves the dimly lit shop to a chorus of 'Thank you, my friend'.

Occasionally I would be reminded of my mother, the cucumber woman, as they called her, by the Habibs. And sometimes I would get Jeff to ask Habib if she still came into the shop. But it seems she either moved away or gave up kebabs nearly twelve years ago, which coincides with the last call she made to me when she spoke mostly to Mrs Smithy. By then I was nearly an adult and there had been no suggestion of me returning to her for years, but I still worried a little that she might suggest I leave the Smithys. My two mothers got along well but Mrs Smithy knew that I had chosen my life with them determinedly but not easily. Even now I glance away or distract myself if we pass the old house I lived in with Diane.

Smithy comes back from watering the plants on the balcony with his empty VB bottle. 'Have you seen that sprig of parsley lately?' he asks me, referring to

Lia, who until recently had been a fixture in our flat and who Smithy called Parsley because he reckoned that, like a garnish, her presence brightened up the fairly ordinary dish that was our home.

I shake my head, not bothering to note the fact that as Smithy and I spend all our time together he'd know if I had seen her.

Unlike Smithy, who has had countless girlfriends during the last few years – so many that he rarely bothers to learn their names let alone record their phone numbers – I went out with Lia, off and on, for nearly three years. She's pretty well dumped me now. I've heard from some of her Russian friends that she is living in Coogee and has a job in a Surry Hills' advertising company. I can't imagine her wanting to give all that up and I can't imagine me fitting in with her new life – like trying to meld a sixties fridge into your new stainless steel kitchen. It has surprised me how little her going affected me. One day, after a period of little contact, she was suddenly uncontact-able, her parents' lack of English making it impossible for me to get any information from them and her friends confiding that she had a new boyfriend, home and job. It had reminded me of when Dave left my mother and me, and I decided to let it go, telling myself the relationship had become routine and was never going to amount to much. I guess I was in like with her, but that's all.

Feeling bad that I'd not kept Smithy updated on this, I nonchalantly wrap up the final episode of the Dec and Lia story for him as he consoles me as best he can – rolling a spliff that will see both of us laughing at me in minutes.

Jeff returns with our lunch just as Smithy and I, amid a haze of smoke, are completing our assassination of Lia's good character, recalling how she got hit in the head at dusk by a disoriented cockatoo and was from then on frightened of all birds, particularly the flapping of their wings.

Presenting us each with our massive yeeros, Jeff digs again into the carry bag. 'I also got some balaclava.'

Neither of us is straight enough to correct him, so we cheerfully thank Jeff for the kebabs and baklava, clearing our makeshift coffee/dining table so we can lay out our spread that drips in the three food groups we favour – salt, sugar, and fat.

'D'ya remember that guy from school, Andrew Seaton? I saw him on my way back from Habib's; he was driving past in a Saab. Guess he'd been to his parents' place.'

Smithy amuses himself. 'Yeah, I've seen him driving around. Sad story, that one. Suffers from yuppieitis, picked it up at a latte bar in Elizabeth Bay. Must have been in the air-conditioning. They all got it, apparently.'

I think about Andrew Seaton, his teeth bright as a 7/11 on a dark wet night and his thick glasses that we'd teased him about, saying that he'd read so much he'd worn his eyes out. It had made me feel slack but also a little worried about my own eyes.

'I guess he's not spending his days watching old *Simpsons* episodes and *Jerry Springer*, gorging on take-away and raising illegal plants in a fucking crummy matchbox.' I snap with a little too much passion, sounding as if I might be defending wankerism.

The mood swing surprises me more than Jeff or even Smithy.

'Growing plants is not illegal, it's the harvesting part that is,' says Jeff, making us sound like farmers bringing in a crop of wheat.

Smithy responds, his teeth full of taboulleh. 'Bullshit. As long as ya don't sell it they don't care.'

I look at them both, my eyes feeling like red has now completely usurped green, and contradict myself for the sake of an argument. 'They don't care at all – long as you're not selling the stuff. Ya can plant it, pick it, smoke it, eat it, fucking wear it. Long as ya don't fucking flog it.' I hope this will be the end of a debate that, like cricket games at Snapper Street, sometimes continues without end with players changing sides effortlessly and often.

'Well, my little buddy,' says Smithy, 'we certainly couldn't have you floggin it, even if we pulled in a bumper stash from our three little plants. Ya look like shit.'

Deciding to avoid a glance in the mirror, I lay on the floor in front of the TV, happy to pass out as Jeff, still making his way though his kebab, loads a tape of recorded Bloopers and Unreal Ads specials and Smithy polishes off the baklava.

Smithy shakes me awake as a re-run of some American sit-com is coming to an end, the guest appearance of a faded movie star, Joan Collins I think or maybe Elizabeth Taylor, announcing that the series was on an irreversible slide. 'Time for a game of Pick the Feel-Good News Item.'

I perk up and shift to the couch, feeling almost straight. Having devised the game, Smithy is umpire as well as a contestant and keeps the record of our selections. The game is ingenious in its simplicity. Each player nominates four possibilities of what might run as the quirky, uplifting post-weather news item. If no one guesses what Channel 10 runs with, we roll our candidates over to the Channel 9 news, half an hour later. The prize, if someone wins, is free drinks at the pub for the whole night's session, paid for by the losers.

Tonight's selections include some perennial favourites – domino-dropping world record attempt; bizarre wedding location like underwater or sky-diving; latest crazy fashions from Paris catwalks;

birth of a panda cub; derelict building implosion; cat or dog rescued from drain or under house; and solar car race or record attempt.

A bunch of bozos crossing the desert on contraptions that weigh less than a Frisbee and wearing hats covered in solar panel cells gives Jeff a well deserved victory in tonight's FGNI contest.

Smithy sets out his joint-rolling paraphernalia to signal we are about to set out for the pub. Grabbing a bunch of leaves that have been drying in the heat on the balcony, he crunches the crispy prongs in his palm and drops them into a mini hand-held grinder, the mull-o-matic, that is our only kitchen utensil besides plastic cutlery. Next, grabbing a cigarette from Jeff and tearing it open, Smithy measures the perfect grass and tobacco mix in our battered tin bowl and, with nimble fingers, rolls a cigarette paper around its prey before licking and sealing the length. Then he creates a roach from a torn strip of old train ticket, and twists the other end of the spliff to form a point ready for lighting.

My eyes start as we hit the late sun and pass the benches where each morning, from my bedroom window, I can see a group of old Serbian men gathered for a morning chat. I spot a dog trying to pick up a soccer ball in its mouth, like a kid trying to take a first bite into a much too big Easter egg that offers no corners, ends or edges. Sometimes you just have to smash something to get a grip of it. The dog gives up and runs to its yard, where the clothes-line is weighed down with hanging slabs of salted meat drying in the afternoon sun.

We amble past the shops that slouch by the train line as the lady closing up Amit's International Unisex Hairdressing Salon, her brown face expressionless like an old wooden house battened down for a cyclone, struggles with the heavy shutters. The posters featuring long-dated styles are faded from years of sun that have left blue the only remaining colour. I assume the dingy shop is not actually the Bankstown branch of a string of worldwide Amit franchises so guess the 'International' part is intended to try and drag ordinary out of its ordinariness. Next door a couple of Vietnamese butcher shops remain open, the meat looking pastel pink in the fluorescent lighting.

Maya is already ensconced at the pub. We join her as Smithy signals three fingers to Stan. 'Anyone win the game?'

Jeff punches the air with a victory jab.

Smithy collects our order just as Maya throws down half a schooner of Coke so Jeff jumps up to get her a fresh sugar cocktail. It's hard to guess how keen Maya is on Jeff – she certainly likes to have him around, pampering her and fetching Cokes, and Jeff is no doubt very fond of Maya, her clear brown eyes, strong face and soft blonde hair a physical match for her feisty and generous spirit. Several times I had skirted the topic of the identity of Maya's baby's father with Jeff. He was reluctant to offer any information which could be interpreted either as a sign he was sworn to strict secrecy, or that he was the father. It was not Smithy's way to badger Jeff and I toed the line.

When Jeff returns with Maya's Coke he complains to Smithy about the new barman, a youngish Greek guy who looks like Russell Crowe. 'When I asked for just a Coke he says, "The milk bar's down the street mate."'

Smithy smiles and tells Jeff that it's just a joke, but the slight has unsettled Jeff, who is used to new people warming to him immediately. But I guess Russell Crowe won't be repeating his mistake: Smithy strides to the bar to give the new guy the option of losing his movie star looks or learning to discriminate about who receives his smart-ass comments. Russell, electing to stay intact, pulls Jeff a VB on the house, one drink that Smithy and I won't have to finance.

6.

While not the most convenient pool of water for Bankstown residents to fall into, Bondi Beach has the advantage of being permanently covered in a selection of chicks from some of Europe's finest chick-producing countries. Maya doesn't mind, as she reckons the Euro-lads are spunks as well. The feast served at Bondi outshines anything The Golden Food Star can muster, though to date only Smithy has managed to score a Euro-snog. Lonely Planet's failure to promote our own particular corner of Sydney means that this kind of smorgasbord is never going to be coming out to us.

It's a hike to the beach from Bankstown, and with Maya driving doubly so. As our designated driver, Maya insists on full autonomy and that means she takes the route she knows even if it means us needlessly traversing the city.

The exact opposite of Smithy, who takes green to mean fast, orange very fast and red a screeching stop, Maya always drives cautiously, her hands set at eleven and one instead of a more comfortable ten and two, as if she expects all green lights to be turning red any second. Her green is your regular person's orange. Smithy drives as fast as an empty STA bus returning to the depot and his combative nature dictates that his stacks generally involve a merging lane. As far as I know, Maya has never arrived on time but she's also never caused so much as a bingle.

Though he has no real need for a car Smithy assumed ownership of the old white VW Passat, its aerial bent in the shape of Australia sans Tasmania, after an all-night pool and drinking session at The Oasis. With less than two months rego left Maya has insisted we make more use of it. Smithy, after hesitating, has agreed that it makes no difference whether we drink and smoke sprawled in the flat or while travelling in a car.

This morning, Jeff needed more encouragement than usual. We really plied him with VBs last night to celebrate his after-the-weather news item victory and his upcoming job interview. But now, at midday, we are on Canterbury Road, where a few hookers have already taken up their positions, one heavily made-up lady of the day, possibly with an interest in travel, electing to stand directly underneath the sign that notes the distances to Canterbury, Newtown and the city.

Smithy, from the backseat, points a spliff at the

sign. 'Fifteen K's to Newtown? Fuck off! It's a fuckin' world away.'

Jeff sits up front, his window arm our left indicator, chatting to Maya as she avoids the car's dodgy second gear – you have to well-and-truly gun it in first before attempting a speedy shift to third. From the back I maintain control of the CD player that Smithy has somehow connected up so it sits under Jeff's seat. Also acquired at the pub by Smithy, the stacker is rather wasted on us and our four CDs, the tracks so familiar to me that at the end of each song, the first beats of the next track automatically come into my mind. We generally start with The Living End, then Green Day and save the classics – Pearl Jam and Nirvana – for later.

We've got the windows down and Smithy and I dangle our non-smoking arms outside, fingers cooling our bodies like those desert hares with their long ears. The car must look as though it is having trouble keeping the contents of its body from escaping.

Maya pushes the car through the city blocks, purposefully taking her time moving off as the lights turn green. We cheer as she annoys the stress heads who beep from behind. But not all her caution is for purposes of antagonising – the brightly coloured bike couriers have Maya spooked as they dart between cars that would ordinarily, on less gridlocked stretches, eat the two-wheelers for breakfast. Smithy assures us that couriering is just an excuse for guys to shave their legs, wear flouro-clothing and jump traffic lights.

'There!' Jeff yells, pointing at a freshly created parking space on the ironically named Park Street. Maya pulls up and positions us for a reverse park.

'What the fuck are you doing?' Smithy yells from behind. 'We're going to the fucking beach – can you see any fucking waves?'

'We're not going to pass up a free space in the heart of the city. It's a sign. Fate.' Unlike us boys, Maya sometimes answers Smithy back.

'It's not free – there's a fucking meter,' Smithy responds, hoping sanity will win out.

'They're always busted – if it's not we'll leave.'

Smithy, snookered, leaps from the back door as Maya completes her park.

'Look's fine to me,' he says to Maya as she joins him at the meter.

'Try and put a coin in,' she dares him.

Smithy replies cautiously, as if he fears being snookered again. 'Well, that would be a fucking waste if it's working and we're not staying.'

'Okay – I'll put ten cents in to see if it works.' Maya fumbles in her pocket for the smallest coin the machine accepts and drops it in the slot. The coin, much to Maya's delight, falls through the machine.

Maya raises her fist and calls to Jeff, waiting inside the car for the judge's decision, 'Let's go shopping!'

Jeff, not wanting to annoy Smithy, manages a weak thumbs-up.

Maya grabs a pen from the floor of the car. 'Who's got some paper? I'll write a note to say the machine took our money and is busted.'

Smithy, tough but a good loser, says, 'Tear a page out of the street directory to write on – one from the North Shore section.'

Maya and Jeff head for the shops after we agree to meet back at the car at one-thirty. Smithy and I set to looking around for a decent pub – one not overrun by yuppies atop stainless-steel bar-stools. We come across a place nestled between a sushi bar full of wankers and a Starbucks full of tourists but, on poking our noses inside we're hit by Phil Collins piping out of the sound-system. We move on.

Appointments and deadlines hardly figure in our lives, so we practically hear the zoom as office drones negotiate their way around us. Others huddle in door-ways conducting secret smoker's business. A bunch of suits, much our age and headed in our direction, shoot Smithy and I looks of disdain. We combat their artillery by firing off glances of pity.

Finally we come across a pub that doesn't cater to just one tribe. The floorboards are dark and weren't laid yesterday and the staff a mixed bag. Not a tight black T-shirt in sight. We saunter through to the eating area so we can order hot chips to go with our VBs.

Sat behind me are a father and teenage daughter, enjoying some quality time, him on his mobile and her listening to a Discman. Next to us are a couple of business types, not in suits but definitely not on their way to the beach. They seem to be discussing hiring a new publicist at the publishing company they work for. The guy is definitely the senior of the two – about forty, with a small, crowded face and the caramel-coloured eyes of a goat. As he talks his lips, wet and slippery, make smacking sounds like small waves splashing against a wall. The woman opposite him wears milky white skin and dark hair so tall even Smithy would have a problem sitting behind her at the pictures. She is attractive and, I sense, not unaware of it. A bit younger than Goat, she spends a lot of her time agreeing with him but has the confidence to argue some points. All the time she is chain-smoking and picking at the tuna salad she has placed on top of a heavy book containing the life of John Steinbeck. No doubt she'll pull out some mints before her first post-lunch meeting to rid herself of the smell of cigarettes and cat food.

Smithy disappears to get our VBs and I tune in on their conversation.

Tall Hair is explaining to Goat that all she wants is someone who can string a sentence together, has read a few books – including ones that have not been made into films – and, most importantly, could pitch an unknown author to a TV chat show or radio producer. It surprises me that it's really so simple to qualify as employment material in any industry that's halfway decent. Surely there's a secret password as well.

'No one I've interviewed can answer me this one simple question: How would you sell the visiting author of a first novel set in the US deep-south to a bright TV producer, barely out of her teens, who has never read a book and never been out of Australia?' Tall Hair's eyes become slits with the wise expression people make as they drawback slowly on a cigarette.

'So what's the answer?' Goat bleats, not pretending to know.

'Well, it's about being creative. It's no use saying you're from Kyle & Deutsch – she's never going to have heard of us – or giving author background or plot descriptions – young Felicity or Tamara at Channel 9 couldn't give a shit. You imply you're from Time Warner, make vague promises about an *Oprah* appearance or a movie. *That* is what pushes the buttons of a Tiffany Smythe-Brown!'

I switch my ears back to local reception when Smithy returns with the beers and the hot chips arrive from the kitchen. We crap on, between mouthfuls of the tomato sauce-basted fries that we use for food, about nothing in particular, happy to pass the time watching the passing parade of city types in the knowledge that shortly we'll be in the water, on the sand, under the sun – and they won't.

We get back to the car to find Jeff and Maya already in the front seat eating mangoes and paw-paws, juice running down their chins and under their T-shirts.

'Gone healthy have we, Mr VB and Ms Coke?' Smithy says.

'Got these from one of the fruit stalls down towards The Quay – Maya started back-grounding me on some of the fruit names and prices too.'

Maya holds up one of those throw-away cameras. 'I took a bunch of photos of the displays so we can help Jeff practise at home.'

Smithy finishes off the film by snapping away at Jeff and Maya as they struggle with their tropical fruits. Then we take off.

Bondi is packed so we park a few blocks back from the beach, our bare feet touching lightly on the hot bitumen as we cross Campbell Parade. A seagull – or a 'rat with wings' as Smithy calls them – joins us on the sprint across the road, narrowly avoiding the wheels of a car. I see Jeff uncross his fingers as the bird appears safely beach-side.

We weave through clumps of baking tourists and locals sporting the sort of sunglasses that are usually only worn by the Australian cricket team. Jeff secures all our cash in the velcroed pocket of his board shorts, commenting on how thoughtful it was of the government to change our money over to plastic notes so that we could take it swimming with us, as Smithy hides the car keys and our coins in Maya's sandshoes.

Soon we are in the warm water, plunging under the waves, seeking each other out as we re-appear after every onslaught. Here in the safety of my friends I think about the days as kids when we would come here in the old limo, Smithy and I spending hours bobbing up and down on the edge of the vast ocean. I remember the day Mrs Smithy sent a lifesaver in to rescue both of us as we pushed into the sea with the older body surfers. Smithy, embarrassed, berated the hapless lifesaver, who reported back to Mrs Smithy that we were both fine.

Smithy still has a go at his mother about this. Bev smiles at me, knowing I haven't complained once and am unlikely to start.

7.

Stuck between night and morning I lie heavy on the bed, too exhausted to sleep, my mind replaying the day's events as I stare at the ceiling which stares right back.

Death usually visits in the dark and silent hours. A phone call at 3 am. But today's arrow came in full view of a shining morning.

Smithy and I had watched Jeff heading toward us from our spot atop the bonnet of the Passat, which Smithy had parked in a loading zone while we waited for Jeff's interview at the fruit stall to end, willing him to remember the answers we'd practised – like replacing his initial response of 'playful' to the describe-your-personality question with 'persevering'. Jeff shot us a beaming smile, even though we were a block away up the road, after farewelling the fruit vendor. He had the job, no doubt about it.

Further down the street a couple of Mormons picked him out – as they usually did, much to his frustration – and set after our mate as he waited to cross George Street.

Hard as Jeff tried to look confident, someone with a life, going somewhere and not just shuffling along the street, he was like a fly on a hook to those crew-cuts in short-sleeved white shirts. The one time Jeff was bypassed by a pair of Mormons he regarded it as a major victory. Market researchers, on the other hand, with their welcoming smiles, clipboards, and boxes to check for your salary bands and education levels, never bothered Jeff – and this bothered him.

He decided to flick today's Mormons by sprinting to the next crossing, looking back to see if they'd given up on their pursuit, and crashing into the base of some dodgy builder's scaffolding, bringing down a storm of cement blocks on top of him. Some of the blocks that bounced off Jeff rolled onto the road causing drivers to spill their coffees or lose grip of their mobiles, one boulder launching itself at a 4WD's window as the driver screeched to a stop.

Smithy got to Jeff just as the last block landed. Our mate's neck was bent sharply toward his shoulder, his eyes seeking out Smithy for reassurance. Silence and noise duelled, Smithy softly telling Jeff's quiet eyes that the blood flowing from his ear was just a cut while the howling sirens descended.

A guy who'd picked up a flying mobile from the

gutter explained to the furniture store on the other end that the lady who was trying to reserve their last Valencia suite was unavailable.

The ambulance slowed as Jeff left Smithy and I – both of us holding a hand – without a word.

I can hear Maya sobbing from Jeff's bed, but no sound comes from Smithy's room. I fear the sadness that has taken him will consume him in silence – that there will be no Smithy come the full morning.

Every happy moment has become a sad moment and everywhere there is no Jeff.

8.

To have gotten to 29 without ever once going to a funeral is a pretty good record, but I would gladly have attended ten funerals of bit-players rather than this one. Those I've lost before have not been to death, and were not Jeff.

I want this over before it begins. Jeff's departure from my life was as quick as Dave's and my mother's – what I dread is the slow loss of Smithy and Maya. We have moved around our tiny flat during the days since Jeff's death as if it were a huge, empty auditorium – paths rarely crossing, voices rarely used, eyes set to blank. Our car has lost a wheel and there is no spare to get us going again.

My image of funerals – processions of cars, slowed to a crawl, lavish flowers and noble words – does not survive the day. Just despair.

Maya drives Smithy, Rat-Boy and me to the cemetery, parking among other cars that rest under the gum trees lining the road that cuts through the fields of death. Jeff's parents and sisters, so unlike their brother with their blonde hair and Sunshine State tans, sit on outdoor stools beside the deep hole assigned to our mate.

I follow Smithy as he makes his way to Jeff's mother and hugs her, the small lady gradually becoming the one doing the hugging, Smithy more lost than I've ever known. We are introduced to the extended family by one of the bronzed sisters who assures the blue-haired aunt that the pregnant Maya and Jeff were 'just friends'.

To Jeff, for whom Smithy, Maya and me were his world, these other people were 'just family'. He picked us out, like I had done with Smithy and Bev all those years ago, and he never left us – not once – until now. Family might come and go but real friends are forever.

By rights the sky should be dark and thick with bursting clouds. Nature does not indulge us, so we wait in the glaring sun, black shadows doubling our number, for the hearse to bring Jeff back to us for just a moment. A pair of female joggers, mousy pony-tails flicking, passes along the road as I hear Smithy sidle up to old Blue Hair, Jeff's nemesis at family weddings. 'You're next.'

While it is not easy to give presents to someone who is gone I guess this to be the first of many fare-well gifts Smithy would make to Jeff.

Rat-Boy sits where Jeff would have if it weren't Jeff's burial we were leaving. Maya drives slower than if we were in a funeral procession but no one complains.

Smithy pulls a joint from his pocket and lights up. I find Jeff's favourite Pez dispenser – Daffy Duck – under my feet, and we pass around the sweets while smoking the spliff. For a moment both Smithy and Jeff are back with us.

We've not been to the pub since Jeff's death but Maya doesn't even bother checking with Smithy as she dumps the car outside The Oasis. If we went into the flat now, we'd sink again. Stan has the VBs and Coke poured before the four of us have sat down. A pretty smart guy, Stan. He joins us and reminisces about Jeff, recalling some of his funny ways – like the questions out-of-nowhere, or how he ate so slowly that we swore even a Big Mac bun would go mouldy as he picked at it.

And about the time Jeff had told the story about Venice, the canals and the vindaloos that plied them. Jeff had laughed loudest when Stan explained they were called gondolas not vindaloos and then Smithy had finally laughed along when Jeff's smile showed he had taken no offence.

Once Stan is back behind the bar and Rat-Boy has gone home, the three of us try to out-do each other with our own Jeff stories. We each want to know everything about Jeff that we might have missed or ignored or forgotten – not just the funny things he did but the sweet things. Like his unrestrained joy at stumbling across, against the odds, a previously unseen *Seinfeld* episode years after the series had folded. While in a way I want to keep some Jeff moments for me alone, it is a fair trade as I'm starving for any stories the others have kept for themselves. It is as if we are trying to soak up a pool of water before it evaporates under the blazing sun, each new story a sponge-worth of life that we can keep forever.

Maya tells us about the time Jeff ordered our food at the Macca's drive-through 'to go'. Tears roll down our faces as she explains how he continued to do it from then on because he knew how much she would laugh.

Smithy counters with the time he went with Jeff to the medical centre, where Jeff complained that he became nauseous when he listened to loud music. 'Then stop listening to loud fucking music,' the exasperated doctor had said. I'd heard this story already from Jeff, who proudly added that Smithy had threatened to break the doctor's fucking face.

I round off the reminiscences with the time I'd gone over to Jeff's as a teenager after Mrs Smithy had sent me to the supermarket with a shopping list that ended with 'pto'. I'd had no idea what pto was, and returned with only half the shopping to much ridicule from Smithy. Jeff, heart as big as an ox, tried to ease my embarrassment by telling me that he would have taken it be an abbreviation for potatoes.

After the pub closes Maya drives home to her sister's place. Smithy and I decide to walk the short distance to our flat and share some more stories. Smithy pulls another joint out of his pocket and we smoke quietly in honour of our lost mate.

As I have done each night since the accident I lie on the bed exhausted, stoned but unable to sleep. My single blue sheet forms waves under which I am drowning. In this flat that the three of us have shared for so long, Smithy and I are now both alone. Tonight though, in the silence, I think about the stories and occasionally an unexpected laugh breaks the quiet.

Awaiting a ray from the morning sun, it comes to me that I have not eaten for twenty hours. Returning from a kitchen alive with mouse activity, I get back into bed and rest a container of chocolate ice-cream on my stomach. As I give the solidly frozen ice-cream a chance to melt my mind returns again to Jeff stories, replaying favourites as often as Jeff would his cherished *Simpsons* videos.

9.

'What the FUCK have you done to yourself?'

Unsure if Smithy is screaming at me in a dream or for real I open my eyes to see him standing in the doorway of my bedroom, a look of total bewilderment on his strong face.

The smell is familiar . . . chocolate. I'm coated, the bed is drenched and even the wall and floor have copped a serve. The empty container and useless plastic spoon have ended up on the floor as well. As my brain moves slowly, Smithy has already sussed what's happened. He's bent over holding his stomach, tears of laughter rolling.

The room looks like a murder scene, but smells like the Cadbury's factory. Smithy's on the floor now, convulsions of hysteria making it impossible for him to remain upright. I'm hoping this is all therapeutic for him as I'm finding it hard to enjoy the mess myself.

'Wasn't it cold sleeping in a bed of ice-cream?' Smithy splutters.

'It was quite a warm night.' I'm starting to smile now.

'You've obviously slept well,' Smithy says quietly, and I suspect he hasn't. I start to lick myself like a cat so I can continue to bask in a happy Smithy.

'You might try the shower dude.' Smithy laughs and takes off as I make out to hug him with my chocolate-coated body.

Smithy looks up from the sofa as I walk through the living room to the balcony. I'm wearing a shirt and have tamed my hair, so it's obvious I'm planning on going out.

'What are *you* up to?' he says.

'Dunno – need some stuff to clean my room and I might try to get a copy of last weekend's paper. I wanna keep a copy of the notice about Jeff that his parent's placed.'

'It's about him being dead – we should have stuff that's about him being alive.'

Smithy's not angry or insistent – just thoughtful – and I decide I'll still try to grab the memento while I can. News of the accident didn't rate the TV or radio as far as I know, and I like the thought of Jeff's name being important enough to be seen by all manner of people, over their breakfast, around the country.

It's already about lunchtime, for those who follow such timetables, when I leave the flat and head off to the shopping strip that seeps underneath the railway station into a cool, dark tunnel that brings you out to more shops on the other side. Not until my third attempt do I find a place that hasn't yet returned its weekend papers. I thank the girl for her inefficiency and head for a spot in the sun, sitting on one of the benches that spring up from the main square around the foaming fountain.

I'm not familiar with the paper's layout, and it takes me a while to find the personal notices. Smithy is right – the section with news of Jeff is under the heading of 'Deaths'. For a second I want to discard the whole paper but decide to tear out the short announcement of his family's sadness in case I regret not having kept it later. There is no mention of who Jeff was, of course, beyond an amalgam of seven and then five letters, his relationship to some still living people he barely rated with when he was alive, and a series of numbers he never chose but is now stuck with: 1.9.73–3.12.02.

The whole lot had been landed on him like the cement blocks. For me, he was Jeff, not Jeffrey Acton, he'd chosen Smithy, Maya and me for his family, and he'll be around far beyond 3.12.02. A photo of his face, a story of his sweetness, news of his job – these should be seen by a million people who would never have noticed him as they rushed to work or the shops.

I decide to see if the job that was Jeff's for the shortest of moments has been advertised – maybe that would be as significant a death notice. Scrolling through the columns and pages of the employment section I stop at a large ad placed by 'Kyle & Deutsch – Publishers'. It takes a second for my brain to recall what my eyes already seem to know. The ad is for the publicity job that I heard Goat and Tall Hair talking about in the city pub. Without hesitating I tear it out and toss the rest of the paper in the bin by the bench. From what seemed like a tree's worth of paper I'm down to two scraps. Both could easily be nothing or maybe everything.

As I stretch out on the bench to contemplate, playfully, the notion of going for a job after all these years, without any resume, in a field I have no idea about let alone any qualifications or experience it occurs to me that Maya's sister, Sascha, works in a book shop at the mall.

I decide to walk the sizeable distance to the mall rather than catch a bus so I can turn back at any time and at no cost. My uncooked plan is to get some background on the publishing and publicity world from Sascha and then decide if I'll take a shot at calling Kyle & Deutsch about the job. My only chance in this fantasy is to bluff my way straight into an interview – any attempt at a resume would be as risible to me as to any prospective employer. If I score an interview I'll have to come up with answers to questions about what I've done since school – a response of 'nothing' might not swing it – and hope that Tall Hair's beloved question about how to sell a first-time foreign author to a young disinterested Australian talk-show producer gets thrown up.

Realising I'm in daydream-land, I stop dead in my tracks. The footpath that runs alongside the highway is full of cracks, weeds growing free along both sides. There is a smooth silver barrier separating the occasional walkers from the hordes in their cars. I've passed no human traffic on the path while the road alongside fairly teems with movement. As I stand facing a future, the sun on my face either calling me on or trying to force me back, I reach in the pocket of my jeans for the job advertisement.

Jeffrey Acton. Much loved son of Malcolm and Barbara Acton and brother of Vicki and Tracey. 1.9.73–3.12.02.

I walk on.

Passing through the express section of the vast mall car park – 90 minutes or less – I make determinedly for the automatic doors. I won't let them ignore me as they did Jeff last time he was here – standing on the rubber mat and staring up at the red beam-light – before opening as Smithy joined him.

The cool of the mall seems to have preserved the inhabitants, who in the main move slowly with glazed expressions. Not sure which book shop Sascha works in, I check out the mall directory that offers clues to those not willing to merely wander: one book shop on the first level and one on the top level.

On my way to the first shop I catch a glimpse of Sascha, taking a break, in the cafe that fills the centre of level one. She's by herself so I saunter in, hoping she'll recognise me before I'm sat at her table.

Sascha is a couple of years older and a few centimetres shorter than Maya but shares the same ash-blonde hair and clear brown eyes. Smithy went out with Sascha for a month or so a year back, not long after her divorce. They parted as friends, which was handy for me now and also made life easier for Maya. The similarities between Sascha and Maya could have you thinking that Smithy must have been interested in Maya at some point. But for Jeff he might've I guess.

'Dec! How are you?' Sascha asks me as I give her a kiss.

'Not too bad.'

'I'm so sorry about Jeff – how's Smithy?'

I sit opposite Sascha and when the waitress comes over I order a coffee for me and another for Sascha.

'He'll be okay – not saying much though.'

'Sounds like Maya. I'm trying to be around for her as much as I can.'

Once the coffees arrive I decide to whip out the Kyle & Deutsch ad and let it explain my not-so-accidental visit. Sascha reads the ad quickly and looks at me.

'Are you going to apply for this?'

There's not a hint of mockery in her voice.

I explain how I overheard the couple responsible for the ad and, insuring myself with a display of 'I don't really care' attitude, go on to describe the farcical scenario in which I might just get an interview and the job.

Not for a second does Sascha doubt the possibilities. Indeed, soon she has me caught up in her enthusiasm.

'I've dealt with the publicists from a bunch of publishing companies when we've had authors in the shop for signings and it doesn't look that difficult,' she says.

I take this in the best possible vein, as it is meant, and listen as Sascha describes in basic detail how the book trade works.

She's right, I think, it doesn't sound impossible.

There's a spring in my step as I say goodbye to Sascha, who has probably lost her job after taking a 45-minute break. The automatic doors have no option but to part for me as I bound through and begin the walk back beside the highway.

The journey home seems a lot quicker and the sun, on my back, is on my side. I look in as I pass the pub hoping that Smithy and Maya have made an early start, and bingo! there they are, sat with Rat-Boy and seemingly in good spirits.

Smithy grins at my pink face. 'Sun, Dec? Let me get you a bevy.'

He sticks one finger up at Stan, who starts to pull a VB for me. When I head to collect it I'm hit on by an attractive Maori-looking girl I've not seen in here before. I feel stupid that I'm unable to muster much charm – opportunities like this are much rarer for me than for the likes of Smithy. We chat for a bit at the bar but that all ends when she asks me if I have someone special in my life and I reply that I'm down to two.

Returning to my mates, Maya, not usually one for interrogations, asks what I've been up to.

'Nuthin much – went to the mall. That's about it really.' I don't want further questions about my recent movements.

Smithy is oblivious and Maya lets it go. Part of me yearns for their approval but I decide to say nothing about the dream job until after I've tried to get an interview.

We spend the night smoking, drinking, playing pool and not talking about Jeff. My eagerness to chase this job has come from nowhere and has unsettled me, but as we spend the night effortlessly together I realise while I want my days to be different I still want them to end up here. Home.

10.

Smithy is sucking on our second joint of the day. I'm being careful not to draw back – I want to remain straight enough to call Kyle & Deutsch at last, the ad having remained in my pocket until deadline day. Now that the living room is no longer a third bedroom the sofa has become home to food containers and loaded ashtrays. Without Jeff to clear the junk off his bed each night, trash-anarchy is setting in.

I've spent the morning lying on the floor. How can I get past the resume requirement and straight into an interview? As each plan takes form I hit the wall of reality that makes the same strategy seem ridiculous. In the end I decide to play it as it unfolds on the basis that it's a long-shot anyway. Let chaos set the course.

As soon as the kebab-aholic heads out I'll make the call. The job ad asks you to email your resume to the Publicity Manager – Tall Hair, presumably. I'll grab her name from the receptionist and go from there.

My anxious expression helps to cover up the fact that I'm totally straight when Smithy finally succumbs to his strongest addiction and heads to Habib's. I dial 1223 to get the number for Kyle & Deutsch and some machine's voice tells me that I've requested the number for Rolls Royce. After objecting, I get a live one.

'I want the number for Kyle & Deutsch,' I say as clearly as I can manage.

'Sorry I don't have a listing for that. I do have a number for a Kyle & Deutsch though.'

'I'll take that, then,' I reply, making sure I copy down the number as this may take a few shots.

'Kyle & Deutsch, Naomi speaking.'

'Hi, can I have the name of your Publicity Manager please?'

'Yes, it's Maxine Clement.'

'Thanks.'

Two minutes, slightly different voice from me, same Naomi.

'Can I have the direct number for Maxine please?'

'What's it in regard to?' Naomi asks.

'Tonight's author event,' Chaos, just in time, replies.

Impressed, or bored, Naomi gives me the number.

Base one secured. A mountain of climbing ahead.

I call Maxine's direct number and get voicemail. It's lunchtime so I decide to give her another five minutes to polish off her tuna and cigarettes. Luckily a stoned Smithy is a slow-moving Smithy so he may just be leaving our block still. Four minutes pass and I press redial.

'Maxine Clement.'

This next bit I've written down in advance, like an acceptance speech for an Oscar. Chaos might need something to work with.

'Hello, my name is Declan, Declan McPherson.' Sascha suggested repeating my name for effect. 'I'm calling in regard to the publicity position. I've literally just arrived back in the country and noticed the advertisement, but I see the deadline is today – and, wouldn't you know, the laptop with my resume has been lost by Qantas.'

'Well, Declan I'm actually between interviews – do you have any experience in books?'

'Mainly overseas, but I'm keen to make Sydney home now.'

Now I have to leave myself at the mercy of the roulette wheel that is spinning under Maxine's tall hair. Base 2 is probably the steepest and most difficult stage, short of the summit. With Chaos as my guide, we endure the pause as the silver ball lands.

'Can you come in for 2.45?'

'Today?' I stutter. 'Of course – your offices at 2.45.'

'I'm actually meeting candidates in the cafe at the front of our building so I'll see you there.' Maxine hangs up.

Fuck, fuck, fuck. My mind is racing. I can forget this now and not front, but somehow the idea of making the day unique by ignoring all the barriers is enticing beyond measure. Knowing that the next few hours hold new, unpredictable experiences is not as debilitating as I'd imagined it would be. But still, the obstacles swirl, attacking my resolve like so many snipers. Lack of clothes, lack of resume, lack of experience, lack of explanation for wasted years since school, Smithy's reaction, and fear of *actually* getting the job!

The best plan I can come up with is to call Sascha at her work. I listen for bemusement in her voice, but even with my radar set to super-sensitive I pick up nothing. Sascha does admit that I'm going to be lucky to cover the fact that I've barely worked since leaving school. Her final advice is to treat the interview as a challenge so extraordinary that achievement through ordinary means and by regular ways is impossible. I'll only get the job if I keep pushing plausibility to the very limits.

I leave the flat and leg it to Sascha's as she's told me I can grab her ex-husband's suit that was at the cleaners when they split. Maya's not home so Sascha has okayed me using the broken front window for entry. Finding the suit, still on a cheap wire hanger and under plastic film in Sascha's closet, I change clothes, leaving my jeans folded on Sascha's bed and make my way for the train station, praying that I don't run into Smithy.

I want to know the ending to this story before

commencing the tale. The dark suit matches nicely with the white shirt and leather shoes I borrowed from Stan for Jeff's funeral and have failed to return. Like so many library books and rented videos. Like me and the Smithys.

On the train I head for the cool of the downstairs compartment so I won't sweat, and start plotting my story – a fiction that can get me through until I get to use the only real ammunition I've got. Off the train my next stop is Tie Rack to buy a strip of silk to wrap round my neck. I go for black to match the suit so that this ensemble of other people's clothes might in some way look coordinated. The lady in the shop kindly ties the noose for me and wishes me luck.

It's a good half-hour before the interview but I've figured it best to allow myself time to acclimatise to the clothes and my story in the unfamiliar environment of the city lest I act like a stunned goldfish thrown in a tank of too-cold tap water.

Finding a coffee shop opposite Kyle & Deutsch's building I sit inside the front window and peek across the road at the café that takes up most of the ground floor and the pavement in front of it. Thanks to the heat of the day the inside section is full of people, but the bright outdoor settings are also nearly chokkas. I try to pick out Tall Hair but can't see her outside.

Presumably she's grilling some candidate in the cool of the café proper.

The waiter takes my order for 'coffee' which, I realise suddenly, is a bit unexotic for a city coffee shop. I'll upgrade to latte or cappuccino when I'm over the road, under the spotlight, out of my mind. The thought of cappuccinos takes me back to one of the Jeff stories we told the night of his burial – how he had ordered a 'cup of chino' once when he was with Maya at the mall. She wasn't sure if he was trying to make her laugh, but he succeeded anyway. I smile as I imagine doing the same to Tall Hair during the interview to see if she'd laugh – or write me off immediately. Thinking about Jeff reminds me how I've gone the whole day without feeling down about him, and the mixture of guilt at forgetting to be sad and the feeling of relief at the easing of the load blends like coffee and milk.

A pile of dark hair across the street catches my attention and I watch as Maxine Clement shakes hands with a suit at the only remaining outdoor setting. The suit is about my age but a perfect specimen of the Aryan race – tall, fair skin, blond spiky hair and, no doubt blue, blue eyes. He carries a brown leather folder that I fear includes all the experience and qualifications that I'm trying to fabricate. Maxine appears to ask him what he'd like to drink and she heads off inside the packed café to place the order.

The Aryan guy checks the sky for the sun's position and sits himself with his back to it.

I decide to spend a minute worrying about the possibility that Tall Hair will recognise me from the pub all those weeks ago. This seems unlikely – as I'm sure Smithy and I would look unremarkable to Maxine and the Goat guy.

I could, of course, make sure of it by doing as Aryan has done and placing Maxine directly in the sun so that she can barely make out my face. She conducts the entire interview with her right hand held above her eyes, the pins and needles no doubt causing her to dismiss Aryan without so much as a handshake.

As I watch Maxine head inside the cool café to scout for a table I pay my bill and spend a last minute running through my thinly constructed work history. I have been, you see, toiling for my fictional father in a fictional bookstore in a fictional American town. I've chosen America so I can draw on the vast bank of data I must have collected from TV. In my head I've formed a life by meshing settings, scenes and characters from *Ellen*, *Seinfeld* and *Friends*. As Sascha says, I have no real hope of getting this job through conventional means.

Ignoring the tightening knot in my stomach and checking the tightness of the knot around my neck I dart across the busy road. Waiting for the green man would give me too much time to sweat. The table Tall

Hair shared with Aryan must remain the only one available – she is heading back outside as I land on the pavement and in the fire. I realise there's no way she'll recognize me as the 2.45 candidate – I carry no folder or bag – and figure that it's up to me to approach her.

'Excuse me, are you Maxine Clement?' I ask as she approaches the empty setting.

'Yes, I am. Declan McPherson?'

'Pleased to meet you.'

I shake Maxine's soft hand. Looking at her so close I remember how milky white and smooth the skin on her face is – like the skin on the inside of your upper arms.

'Would you like a drink?' she asks.

Don't say a cup of chino.

'A latte – thanks.'

She goes back inside and I sit myself in the seat she had previously occupied. The sun stings my face. I smile thanks as she places two lattes on the table and sits in the relative shade of Aryan's seat.

Maxine scans our otherwise empty table for my brown leather presentation folder and I decide to distract her from questions about references and resumes by launching into my background story. I stretch the bits that feel most comfortable as I hope to leave Maxine less time to ask probing questions – well, any questions outside the one that I specifically count on her asking.

'... and then I decided to leave my father to run the store by himself and I've just, as you know, arrived back in Sydney. Still waiting for my luggage, wouldn't you know!' I give a knowing shrug – who'd ever trust an airline?

Continuing to masquerade as Mr Confident I launch my next offensive – which in reality is a retreat designed to avoid answering questions. 'Can you tell me some more about this specific position you have available?' I try to sound animated, as though I've not practised the question a hundred times in my head already.

Tall Hair, relaxed with the sun off her face, explains the set-up of the publicity department. She's manager, some guy she calls 'Mate' is senior publicist and there are two junior publicists – and looking for a third.

'You would be responsible for some fiction and the lifestyle titles and after a time you'd take over the MBS books.'

I nod knowingly, sweat running down my chest and stomach, the fear of a specific question on MBS driving me to up the risk factor.

'Cigarette?'

Maxine looks me square in the eyes as I pull my packet of durries from the pocket inside Sascha's ex-husband's ex-jacket.

Her relief is palpable. 'Yes, please.'

I assume Tall Hair to be at least a pack-a-dayer. These back-to-back interviews must be playing havoc with her smoko schedule. Offering the packet to her I remember to keep my thumb over the skinny joint that sits among the regular cigarettes. I'd prepared the spliff for my walk from the station later this afternoon either in celebration or – most likely – consolation. When you're bobbing around in uncharted territory it's reassuring to have a familiar event planned: the walk from Bankstown train station with a joint was my safety rail.

As I light Maxine's cigarette and my own I glance to the next table for a time check on the wrist of one of the suits. Twenty minutes have passed. I probably haven't advanced my cause, but the greater victory is having not yet blown myself out of the water.

'What are you reading at the moment?' Maxine asks in such a way that I'm unsure if we we're still in interview mode or just chatting in a fag break.

I decide to keep up the momentum. 'Grapes of Wrath – again!' I lie.

The sun has sunk behind the top floor of the gigantic building across the street. I can see Maxine now and this answer has scored well.

She leans forward, eyes focused. 'Can I ask you a pretty tough question?'

'Of course,' I say as calmly as I can manage.

Maxine loads a bullet into one of the empty chambers and points the gun right at me. 'How would you sell the visiting author of a first-time novel set in the US deep south to a bright young commercial TV producer, barely out of her teens, who has never read a book and never been out of Australia?'

I give a thoughtful look as my brain searches for its much-rehearsed answer. Trying not to grin I lean forward to meet Maxine's face over the centre of the table. 'If she is so young and inexperienced I would prefer to play down the pitch on company or author but instead would talk about the real possibility that the author might, say, appear on *Oprah* or have the book optioned as a movie. I'd chuck in names for lead roles – Keanu Reeves and Reese Witherspoon, say.'

A shot of fear races through me. Was that *too* similar to the 'perfect' one she had told Goat in the pub? But Maxine draws back in her seat and smiles as if she were the one who just hit a six.

Desperate to end on a high note I look around for the next candidate. A pretty Chinese girl hovers nearby, balancing a stack of presentation folders. I nod in her direction to Maxine, stand and stretch out my hand. 'Thanks for the interview, Maxine. Can I give you my number or should I call you?'

'Please give me a call tomorrow afternoon, Declan. I should have made a decision by then. It's been a pleasure to meet you.'

I leave with a smile for the overloaded Chinese girl. 'Good luck!' I say as she struggles over to my still-warm chair.

The train trip back to Bankstown is long enough to allow me to recount the interview about nineteen times. I'm smiling so brightly that nobody dares sit next to me.

Finishing the spliff I dive through Sascha's front window and switch back into my jeans, leaving the suit to hang on its wiry shoulders. I decide to head home to fill Smithy in. It all means nothing without him along, and soon we'll be at the pub with Maya and Rat-Boy taking stabs at what the fuck MBS might be.

11.

'... and from next season the Mind Body Spirit titles.'

Maxine, aka Tall Hair, solves the great mystery of MBS while she runs me through a long list of responsibilities. It's my first day at Kyle & Deutsch. I try to remember as much as possible but it's hard to imagine that the jargon and acronyms will ever make sense to me. And if I ask for definitions, I'll only draw attention to my total inexperience. Like a street person who has snuck into Tiffany's I await the inevitable polite ejection – but hope to enjoy the sparkle from at least one diamond before being discarded. Maxine, fortunately, seems like a busy lady. She doesn't stop to ask me questions, just cruises through the preliminaries. Maxine's office holds the high-ground in the warren of hutches that fill the valleys of Level 34 in the crisply designed Universal Tower. Her room is attached to the long clear window that wraps itself neatly around each floor, revealing an outside world to workers of rank.

'Do you have any questions before I show you around?' she asks.

I'd like to know if Smithy is up yet and if he's okay. I want to know if tonight at the pub can be the same when the day that precedes it has altered so dramatically. Can Maxine explain my feeling that life has to change now that Jeff is gone? Will I ever meet a girl who will be satisfied with what is enough for me? What is her opinion on the odds of me surviving a day, let alone longer, in this world?

Maxine ain't God, so I ask instead if there is a cafeteria.

Her face tells me that isn't quite what she had anticipated. 'Yes there is, but I meant do you need any more information about your role here at K&D?'

'Nope, I think it's all pretty clear,' I say from the fog.

I think about Smithy, now alone in the flat. Probably he'll smoke a few cones by himself and then later fetch a kebab and follow up with a chick (or maybe two) if there is any fit talent hanging around Habib's.

I left the flat as late as I could, spending the money Maisie had given me for my birthday on a taxi, hoping to the last minute that Smithy might join me for a pre-work spliff. He took the news well when, three weeks ago, I called Maxine from the flat for her verdict. I'd been so stunned by her thumbs-up that I forgot any plans for breaking the news gently to Smithy. The sound of an era ending is silence, but it sure packs a punch.

Given that as an experience a taxi-ride is up there with trying to remove your own teeth, it seems weird that taxis are so expensive. Mario, with his extravagantly styled hair, decided I needed to know his name and other vitals – divorced, living in Leichhardt, morning shift six days a week. When he tuned his radio to some talkback fascist plying his ugly trade, I took to looking in on other people's lives. A couple in a BMW gazed silently out their respective side windows, the woman passenger so longingly applying hand cream it was almost erotic. Noise or silence – it's hard to select the right station sometimes.

Mario dropped me off directly in front of the café and with hundreds of others I marched toward the towering office block, slowing through the revolving doors and heading through the foyer to the bank of lifts.

Level 34, nearly at the top of the building, was already lit on the lift's inner display panel. I scanned the packed box wondering which of my fellow astronauts was a co-worker. Some of the crew were preening themselves in the mirrored back-wall, but I had no opportunity to check my own look in privacy.

As our number thinned with the air, I realised

that my companion bound for Level 34 was the Goat guy. Panic rose, but in his caramel eyes there was no hint of recognition – not even as we abandoned the lift in tandem, me lingering a little so I could follow as he charged past reception.

The receptionist meanwhile had just answered the phone by welcoming the caller to Microsoft, so it was fair to assume she was either holding down a second job or taking a long time to forget a previous gig.

'Okay – let me introduce you to the team.' Maxine fingers quotation marks around 'the team', which I find ominous.

I follow her out of her office and along a corridor flanked by windowed offices down one side and a maze of partitioned spaces on the other. Most of the offices have their doors closed. We turn into the maze and stop at the first cubicle. So this is where 'the team' play the game.

'Declan, this is Maet – M, A, E, T – our Senior Publicist, your immediate report. Maet, this is Declan McPherson.'

Maet is much my own age and I'm surprised by the relief I feel that my boss is not younger than me. We shake hands and Maet offers a smile – the first I've scored today.

'Okay, Declan. I'm going to leave you with Maet

now. He'll introduce you around and get you settled at your desk.'

Maxine stalks off as Maet gestures for me to follow him to a group of three hutches, each half the size of his.

'Declan McPherson, this is Naomi Bracewell and this is Naomi Anderson. They are our other two publicists.' He spins on his heels to point at the empty desk among the three. 'And this is your spot.'

Both the Naomis are wearing black. Naomi Bracewell is barely twenty, I guess, with soft dark ringlets of hair and brilliant blue eyes that immediately make you suspect she wears coloured-contacts. Naomi Anderson has no hair at all, but her head is loaded with rows of silver earrings in both ears as well as one that holds her left eyebrow in place. She is skinny and angular, as if she might break if squeezed too tight, but a permanent smile contradicts the severity of the rest of her look.

Maet, reading my mind, says, 'We tend to call these guys Naomi A and Naomi B to avoid confusion. He smiles. 'Oh, and you saw the receptionist? She's Naomi on Reception.'

The publicity Naomis spend the rest of the morning showing me where everything is housed: the copies of books to be sent to reviewers and media people, the clippings received of reviews done, the lists of reviewers and book information kept on computer – how am I going to handle that?

And then, at last, the cafeteria. With prices heavily subsidised by other, more benevolent companies that occupy Universal Tower, the tenth floor cafeteria's only drawback is that K&D employees are not officially welcome.

Naomi B explains that we need only linger outside the security door on Level 10 for a minute until someone with a security card comes by for their lunch. We'll cruise in in their slipstream.

Soon we've followed a gaggle of security-ignorant office types into a scene from an American high-school movie: lots of ladles, individual portions and faux-wooden trays sliding around on silver tracks like scalectrix race-cars controlled by a kid with a nervous trigger finger. Momentarily I consider telling Smithy and Maya about this place but decide that after my imminent ditching from K&D I'll hardly want to return to eat lunch, however cheap, surrounded by these legitimate workers.

Over lunch, Naomi A rests her silver-laden ears and fills me in on as much office gossip as she can manage in an hour.

'She might look good, but whatever you do don't fuck Virginia in Accounts.'

I just nod as if she is telling me to keep the press

clippings alphabetised by author surname. It's highly unlikely I'll meet the infamous Virginia before I'm given the heave-ho for impersonating a publicist. Naomi A is plainly looking for a soul mate, but I'm too wary to say much.

My self-appointed guide continues with her run-down but the names and roles are all a blur except for 'Maxine' and 'Maet'. All the while Naomi B has her impossibly blue eyes beamed on the screen of the funky mobile she grips with both hands, her right thumb dancing over the tiny keys as she no doubt texts her friends updates on her life.

After lunch the Naomis deposit me back to Maet, who – thank goodness – takes it upon himself to log me into my computer, then issues me with a mobile phone no larger than a Tim Tam. He even sets my chair while I try to upload the steps involved in getting the lap-top going into my own brain's hard drive.

Maet's attitude as he explains the procedures in the publicity department seems pretty casual and I feel that he is not going to be overly concerned by my initial ineptitude. I decide to take notes as he runs through the places of interest on my screen, and he doesn't blink when I've written nearly twenty pages by the end of what he had assumed was an informal briefing.

Each time he asks me whether I know this email package or that version of Windows, I have to shake my head and imply that I'm more familiar with another. None of this fazes Maet, who might just enjoy the fact that I'm not a know-it-all while unaware I'm a know-nothing.

My note-taking slows as I become familiar with new words that seem common in this new environment. Mostly these are three words that act as one: 'doubleclickon', 'alloneword' or 'heorshe'. For the life of me I can't guess why there's an A, C and D drive but no B, but I choose not to ask in case it's obvious.

We spend the rest of the afternoon in my interview café, Maet chain-drinking black espressos and, his dark eyes animated, talking about books the way others speak about TV or movies, but not saying much about work. I'm on steadier ground here and start to relax, my first day nearly complete with no real glitches – no real work either, though.

It occurs to me that one of the tasks I had set myself as I lay in bed early this morning, running through a hundred scenarios where I might come a cropper, was to note the dress code. Today I'm wearing the interview outfit again. Tomorrow I'll be in a bind if I need anything above street-grunge. Maet's black hair is unruly and he hasn't shaved since at least last Friday, at a guess. I can manage that look, but how will I manage his dark, slim-fitting pants with a Hugo Boss tab and designer black T-shirt?

Out the front I can see Goat sitting with one of

his staff. Goat wears more traditional business attire, while his underling's reflector sunglasses no doubt allow Goat to look into his own yellowed eyes for the duration of their meeting.

Outside the cafe a familiar sight makes me realise how much I relish a familiar sight. The Passat has landed directly out front of Universal Tower, which has commenced reguritating the humans it consumed during the day. Maet, noting my distracted face, sees me off with a 'See ya tomorrow, dude' and I throw myself into the battered car, Maya and Smithy both grinning at me.

'Where to, Mr Worker man?' Smithy asks, imitating that non-existent species, the polite taxi driver.

'Hugo Boss, if you please.'

12.

We don't bother checking the parking signs or meters. With the increasingly incapacitated Passat now just a couple of days from being out of rego and who knows whose name on the rego papers, Smithy has decided that if the car gets a ticket we'll just remove anything we want and catch a train home.

Having de-suited in the back seat, changing into the old jeans and T-shirt that Maya has brought along, I am again me. Dec.

A street person, who appears not to have de-suited in a while, paces by the crossing that will take us to the designer shops gracing the opposite side of the road. He rests his bulging bags of possessions against the crossing post and glances across the street to a glamorous lady who is ferrying nearly as much stuff as he has in bags named Gucci, Prada and Hermes. As the rapid fire of the crossing alarm drills he stays behind, content to wait on for a better moment to launch himself, the thumb and forefinger on his raised right hand pressed together like he's some wise figure from a golden Renaissance painting.

The three of us stride into Hugo Boss, confident that we'll be left alone to browse. In the split-up of Jeff's wallet, Smithy had taken his ATM card, Maya his expired driver's licence, Rat-Boy his video card and I his, and our, only credit card. Jeff's father had organised the card for him years back and we had all used it at different times in different binds, the bills, addressed to Jeff at our flat, somehow being met by one or all of us before the card could be cancelled. The cards were dealt by Smithy the night of Jeff's burial, each of us taking our small piece of Jeff without a word.

In consultation with Maya, our unlikely fashion guru, I decide to go with a look more similar to Maet's than Goat's. My big fear, of course, is that my fellow publicists will be wearing a differently labelled ensemble every single day. While I can't afford this early to appear completely out-of-my-depth, I decide to worry about what I'm going to wear one day at a time. There is no reason to buy a month's worth of clothes when this charade seems most unlikely to last out the week.

As Jeff I sink nearly one week's wages into two pieces of labelled black. Four more days of avoiding the inevitable just to pay for one day's get-up.

We dump the new clothes in the boot of our as-yet-un-ticketed car and decide to make the most of the lingering summer afternoon by sharing a spliff down at The Domain while watching office workers play twilight cricket. Apart from a dozen or so nine-to-fivers enjoying a game of hit and run in the centre of the lush playing fields the tree-bordered park is empty.

Maya is now too pregnant to be comfortable sitting on the ground so we make our way to a park bench that has been dedicated to some dead politician who was important in the seventies, in his seventies. The fresh bronze plaque, screwed into the centre of a teak plank and having drawn the long day's sun to it, scalds Maya's upper back like a hot plate. If it weren't for her quick reflexes I could see the flesh between Maya's shoulders being branded with this particular politician's name and short bio until she was likewise dead.

Smithy and I lay on the grass at our pregnant friend's swollen feet, staring directly into the thin clouds above and sharing a joint back and forth – two drags and pass. On the grass, on the grass, under the clouds, under the clouds.

One wisp has made the effort to shape itself as a rabbit. I watch the contorting bunny as its ears lengthen and its face pushes forward in the breeze. Soon enough, it has left its tail behind and is no longer a rabbit.

'So how was it?' Smithy finally asks.

'Well, I've still got the job but there has to be more to it. Once whatever it is needs doing, who knows?'

I don't want to like the job too much yet as it's so fragile and precious that to count on it will surely make it disappear.

Maya leans over. 'What are the people like?'

'The chicks are mostly called Naomi, the ones I've met anyway. Maet, the senior publicist, seems relaxed though I bet he comes from a posh background – right family, right schools, right neighbourhood. Naomi A reckons he's a vampire, though he doesn't seem it. Everyone in publicity wears black, drinks black and probably pop all colours. But hey, look at us.'

'A vampire?' Maya asks the question on behalf of Smithy and herself so that he needn't concede he doesn't know something.

'Yeah, you know. The sort of person who parties all night and spends daylight hours recovering. Nightclub stamps on the inside of their wrist provide their only clues to where they've been the previous night.'

I sink in the grass and contemplate my second work day. I'll be dressed in black like the others, our internal differences strengthened by outward uniformity. Unlike the houses, streets, clubs and malls of Sydney, where sameness pervades both outside and in, it seems with people the less window dressing the more window. Milk cartons are blue and white, salt and vinegar chip packets are purple, chicken green, and publicists are black. It's what's inside that counts.

I prop myself on my elbows and glance around. Maya is now asleep on the park bench, and Smithy also has his eyes closed though I doubt he is sleeping. There's a frown across his strong face, and I guess he's consumed by thoughts of Jeff. His happiness constrained like a cat with a bell around its neck trying to hunt for birds. I nudge him so that the frown will forget why it's there and he whacks me back.

Tonight we'll collect the car if it has escaped a ticketing, argue and laugh as Maya drives us back to Bankstown and load up on kebabs and bevies at Habib's and The Oasis. To always have this – Declan at work, Dec with his mates, this day and forever. I just need a white cat to cross my path.

13.

Theory has it that the train is quicker than the bus, of which I'd have to take several, but I still set off for the railway station well before morning normally nudges me awake.

Smithy has rolled me a commuter spliff and left it by my toothbrush. I grab the joint and ditch thoughts of a no-doubt fruitless search of the kitchen for a real breakfast. Overnight someone has spray-painted graffiti, tribal tags, in a myriad of colours, all over Maisie's next-door neighbour's old Valiant. Knowing Beryl I imagine she won't bother having the car re-sprayed, preferring the looks she'll get – a frail elderly woman, dressed in her immaculate white bowls ensemble – behind the wheel of her garish tank. In Bankstown, it seems the hoonier you are, the bigger the car.

Closer to the station a guy in a tiny red Fiat with a 'Magic Happens' sticker is doing his second lap of the roundabout. No doubt he's trying to find the exit to the eastern suburbs. Small cars like his are as rare in Bankstown as cars with two functioning brake lights.

My face smarts from a second consecutive day of shaving but the sun casts a happy glow and my first thought of Jeff, triggered by the sign on the window of the local Chinese restaurant offering a 'Smorgasbroad', brings a smile. Good morning, Jeff. I walk to the end of the platform to enhance my odds of getting a seat: the suited lemmings, I learn, prefer to crowd into the middle carriages.

Stop by stop my carriage fills, but the seat next to me remains empty. This snubbing would have severely bugged Jeff, but I put it down to the blackness of my clothes. A sheep in wolf's clothing.

The woman across from me has her eyes closed. I decide to stare intensely at her. Can I will her awake? She holds out for a good minute but eventually succumbs, and I quickly pretend that I've been looking at the commuter warning posters above her head. The 'No Drinking' one features a picture of a cocktail glass with a red slash through it. These trains have seen a lot of boozing but I doubt many martinis have been guzzled in Carriage 4273. Two old ladies, arm in arm, make their way to the last empty seat in the carriage – the one beside me – but when one of them affronts the other by offering the seat to her they shuffle off bickering.

I passively inhale a durry and a half as I walk the couple of blocks from the station to Universal Tower among office workers lighting up their first for the day. In the lift my only companion beyond level 27 is a sharply-dressed young woman. Level 34, in addition to Kyle & Deutsch, also houses the suites of the Office for the Empowerment of Women. Maet's advice was if the woman is from K&D stand back, but if not push ahead. Given my co-traveller's suit is not black I decide to win her over by nearly knocking her down.

Naomi on Reception is reading fashion magazines, devouring the ads while flipping past the articles. She barely notices me, let alone my new clothes, so I walk by and deposit myself at my desk.

And so, what now? I turn on the computer and grab my notes. Maybe they'll tell me how I'm going to fill the next eight hours. Neither Naomi A or B is in yet but I can see Maet at his desk – dressed in exactly the same clothes he had on yesterday, which means pretty well exactly what I've got on today. At least I won't have to freak out about what to wear tomorrow, I think, then notice his hair is completely different today, parted on the side and slicked down.

Computer working, I'm alarmed to see that I've received two emails – both from someone I've not yet encountered. The first is titled 'Vermin' so I cautiously double-click the envelope open. Someone called

Emma has decided to announce to the 'Everybody' list that unless people clear up after themselves in the kitchen the mice that had until recently run rampant will surely return. Emma has also lost a tub of blueberry yoghurt that has her name on it and she is expecting a replacement to appear in the fridge by day's end. I suspect that the yoghurt loss is the real reason for the blanket note and possibly also the inspiration for the email's title. To further enforce her determination for rectitude Emma signs off with a confident EMMA.

Emma's second missive is more amiable, written in her capacity as Goat's assistant rather than kitchen vigilante. Entitled 'Agenda' it provides the following cryptic clues to a meeting scheduled for this morning to which a bunch of people are expected to attend including Maxine, Maet, Naomis A and B and myself:

1. Kostya Tzu
2. Lucinda Waterstreet novel
3. Beauty Naturally
4. The new Katz
5. Mango Days
6. Other Business

Maet comes by the hutches to collect me for my first Marketing Meeting.

'G'day little buddy,' he smiles, looking briefly at my near-identical clothing. 'Naomis A and B are both with authors today so it's just you and me to fight the good publicity fight.'

'Hhhhmmnn!' Maxine snorts from behind, in the manner of Marge Simpson. If only her tall hair were blue, her skin yellow and fingers eight.

'Sorry, and of course our fearless leader,' Maet responds.

I'm unsure if I should be intimidated by Maxine but decide I'll tread with caution a while yet. Her bony frame and translucent skin, which make the outline of her skull quite visible, are nevertheless sturdy enough to hold the great head of hair that sits today in a severe bun. If it weren't for the rules of gravity I'd think she was a hair-do with an emaciated body hanging underneath.

'Declan, I hope Maet didn't instruct you on what to wear.'

'Pure coincidence,' I say lightly – not sure myself if that is strictly the truth.

She flashes a smile stronger that you'd believe a diet of cigarettes and bread sticks was able to sustain. 'Difference between men and women number 104. If two women turn up in the same clothes they avoid each other like the plague. Two guys, on the other hand, might just become lifelong friends.'

We walk in a line toward the boardroom, where a wider selection of darkly dressed publishing people have gathered, settling into the cold black and chrome chairs that have been rolled into equidistant positions around an immense faux wooden table. Other than Maxine and Maet I only recognise Goat. The other ten or so people all take a brief moment to look at me without committing to acknowledgement.

I wonder about the assembled group, a few I barely know and the rest not at all. If I'm still at this place in a few months who will make me smile, who will I never forget? I think about the first time I met those who hold my heart now. Smithy, Maya, Jeff – in each case initial impact was minimal, I had no awareness that I'd commenced the slow unwrapping of one of the great prizes of my life. Those that burned brightest on impact, who offered everything at first – Diane, Dave, even Lia – their promise always seemed to fade as the illusion of perfection that I forced upon them became impossible to maintain. Gone forever, lost to me.

Maxine next to me is motioning for everyone to take their seats. What do I know of her? What's to know?

New people always underwhelm Smithy but with me it seems change is inevitable: hot to cold, cool to warm, frost to boil. Jeff reckoned we are all like Kinder Surprises – any of us might contain great joy for someone who need only select us, unwrap and bite. Anyone Jeff met was immediately placed atop one of his forest of pedestals until time-as-lumberjack came to disappoint. Smithy, on the other hand, only granted tickets to his show once most people had tired of waiting for permission to enter.

I swung between the two as I sat there, hoping that now and then the hares just might not slow down but glad that tortoises occasionally hit their stride when you least expect it.

14.

'That's not fucking five bucks worth of chips!'

And so, nearly a decade ago, Smithy made himself known to the girl who had brought our communal lunch to the flimsy aluminium outdoor setting that we'd claimed outside the only kebab shop in Bankstown he, Jeff and I had never yet visited. Though the blonde girl looked a couple of years younger than us she didn't seem at all intimidated by Smithy. I guessed that the shop was a family concern. Inside, behind the counter, a middle-aged couple hacked away at rotating towers of meat, while outside, working the street furniture with our waitress, strode an almost identical but slightly older looking girl. Intriguingly for a fast-food joint specialising in the art of yeeros, the family looked more Serbian than Turkish or Lebanese.

Ignoring customer dissatisfaction, the girl who'd ferried her mother's interpretation of five dollars worth of chips asked Smithy directly if he'd like to order anything else.

'I guess we'll need to – beef kebab, just meat.'

'Lettuce, tomato, onion?'

Smithy responded politely. 'Nope. Just meat thanks, and garlic sauce.'

The girl looked at Smithy with a hint of a smile. 'My father won't appreciate last-minute changes to the order.'

Smithy's trick to make sure he got loads of meat on his kebab, with a new person or place, of asking for just meat then once it is portioned saying 'Oh I think I will have some salad after all' had been torpedoed.

On returning with the kebab – which, to be fair, was bulging with shaved beef mix – the girl sat on the fourth chair without being invited and watched bemused as Smithy unrolled the warm pita bread so Jeff and I could pick out some of the filling.

Jeff immediately commenced interviewing the girl, who happily answered his questions while fending off mental vibes from impatient customers whose signalled pleas for napkins or such were being ignored. Soon it was confirmed that this was her parents' shop and her name was Maya. The other waitress, her only sister, Sascha, worked in a bookshop during the week, but Maya worked all seven days in the family business. It was pretty clear that Maya envied our inability to explain how we spent our days.

Over the next few months this place became our regular yeeros filling station, Jeff in particular showing a new found enthusiasm for leaving the flat that he spent so much time in, though not yet as an official resident, to collect our lunch. However, as Jeff's interest in Maya became increasingly apparent the servings of meat doled out by her father became ever skimpier until Smithy decided to wean Jeff off this particular establishment in case we starved. The only option was that along with our custom Maya also left the Rowan Street kebab shop.

15.

Three chairs around the enormous boardroom table remain rider-less, presumably reserved for a couple of Naomis and one other absentee. People subject the other chairs to swivelling, height adjustments and repeated rolling back and forth. Maxine, Maet and I have grabbed the window side of the table so remain viewless but glare-free.

Goat, opposite us, leads off. 'Good morning all. Special welcome to Declan McPherson, the new junior publicist. No doubt Maet has brought you up to speed on what happens at our marketing meetings.'

He hasn't.

I nod.

Maet gives me a thank-you kick under the table.

'Good. Okay – Emma, can you take us through the items.'

Emma, author of 'Vermin' and 'Agenda', is sitting next to Goat. As she sets about proceedings, her multi-coloured fingernails sparkle, brightened further by the mid-morning sun that streams across the boardroom table stopping suddenly on her, Goat and three others. Emma's short spiky hair and long soft eyelashes are unnaturally black, blue-black. Blacker than the blackest of clothes in the meeting room.

'Item 1 – Kostya Tzu.' Emma holds up what she refers to as a 'mock-up jacket' – a working cover for a book on the Russian-Australian boxer.

With all eyes on Emma, Maet takes the opportunity to slide me a hastily drawn map-o-gram of the table showing stick figure people arranged around it. A smiling sun sits behind Maet's artistic interpretation of our publicity team – the most noticeable feature a massive ball of squiggle that represents Maxine's hair. Maet has labelled the side opposite us 'Marketing', the end to our right is 'Sales' and opposite them is 'Publishing'. Due to time constraints Maet has decided to signify seniority in each team by a ball of squiggle upon the head. And so in the diagram Goat also sits under a Maxine-inspired ball of swirls, as does the middle stick figure in the sales team. In the publishing team, it is the player closest to the door.

I look up from the sketch so that I can match real faces to the figures. In reality the sales manager does not have a massive beehive hairdo – his unruly sun-bleached hair falls from his head and over his eyes like Kurt Cobain's did. He looks like he'd be more comfortable riding the boardroom table across the face of a six-metre wave than sitting behind it being chilled by office air-conditioning. Kurt's light tan looks more significant against the rest of his Goth-pale team either side of him. In defiance of everyone else in the room he is dressed in anti-black: blue flannelette shirt, bright canary-yellow T-shirt and too-big jeans.

The publishing manager is older than the three other senior people in the room. Her face is gentle and uncluttered by make-up. I imagine she covers her mouth to sneeze even when alone. Though short, she hasn't bothered to hoist her seat higher than necessary and sits softly studying the jacket of the Tzu book. On first impression you'd reckon she got to her position as a result of talent rather than aggression. She's a picture of efficiency – her black shirt and pants are unfussy, her short, delicately greying hair is parted on the side and wrapped behind her ears, and her fingers bear no rings, polish or signs of biting. But from this elegant mouse the frank, succinct publishing-speak that Maxine is so adept at, comes out.

'Rags to riches, humble achiever, steely determination and grit, triumph over adversity, shallow waters run deep, yadda yadda yadda ...' the publishing manager summarises the book for all with a string of clichés and one-liners.

'Sounds great – looks dreadful. Red books don't sell, green neither for what it's worth.' Kurt offers a sales perspective. The interim jacket has a lurid red background with a montage of photographs of

Kostya Tzu in winning poses. 'Nipples or snakes on jackets are also the death,' Kurt continues unencouraged, giving me the tip.

'How fat is this epic going to be?' Goat bleats.

'At this stage it's more of a pamphlet,' the publishing manager responds serenely. 'There's a book in him, we just have to get it out.'

Maxine weighs in regarding the publicity possibilities. 'I hope Kostya is going to be a little more available than that trendy fucking cricketer who will remain nameless. If I had to autograph another one of those fucking promotional mini-bats I would have started signing them simply as Fuckwit.'

'Not a problem. We'll have him for three weeks solid, no other commitments,' our PM confirms.

On behalf of the marketing team Emma wonders aloud if we might just get a quote noting the perceptive and poignant writing style of Kostya, who has insisted on doing the book without the help of a ghost writer. 'It would give the book, especially if it's a little slim looking, a bit more cred.'

Everyone agrees and Emma is charged with writing a nice one-liner that she can run past the few sporting celebrities who might make a difference to sales – Eddie McGuire, Les Murray, and Bruce McAvaney – and are credited with some measure of reading ability. The idea, I presume, is that she'll get one of them to read the quote back to her.

Not to be outdone, Kurt further reveals his grunge origins by suggesting a telegraph-pole poster-blitz – with posters flogging the book but created to resemble boxing-fixture promotions. Everyone nods enthusiastically and I warm to the general acceptance of all the varied suggestions.

Goat rises to the challenge. 'Who will we get to stick up the posters? It's not exactly legal.' He's the realist, I twig. And wary of marketing ideas from outside his own department.

'Just ask anyone in Newtown,' Maet suggests and Emma records another marketing strategy in the minutes.

Endeavouring to wrap up item 1, Goat summarises the required information. 'Okay – month, price, quantity?'

'Nine months, we're looking at it handling $29.95 in paperback – can we say 15,000 copies?' the PM asks Kurt's side of the table.

'How many did we end up doing of the Cathy Freeman bio?' Kurt flings the hot potato back to the PM.

'About twelve and a half.'

'D'ya reckon Kostya's bigger than Cathy?' Kurt has waited until the business end of discussions. This might prove to be a good strategy in a game that increasingly resembles *The Price is Right*.

'Probably a tad bigger – Fathers' Day and all that –

but most likely we'll do less than Paul Keating or Pat Rafter. We had 50K of Bradman ready to roll the day he dropped, awaiting final dates and some eulogies, but he was in an entirely different league,' says the PM. I make a note to check the website – all these names, all these books.

'How did that bio you guys did of the Queen go?' Kurt says, still avoiding a definitive number for Kostya Tzu.

The genteel PM looks confused. 'We don't have a bio of the Queen.'

A short silence and the PM's assistant perks up from within the shadows, 'The book titled *Queen: The Full Story* is about the band Queen.'

'Oh.'

'The only other title on our biography list is *A Biography of Time*.' The PM tries to wrap up the procrastinating.

Kurt has used up all his question cards and decides to play his hand. 'I reckon Kostya is as big as time and we did about 17 and a half of that so yeah let's print about 20, with a blue jacket.'

'Done. Item 2 – untitled, Lucinda Waterstreet,' Emma chirps, reminding me that even though my head is awash with a thousand new terms already we still have a ways to go.

16.

'How about this way?' Jeff suggested, turning the old blue couch that he and Smithy were dancing with until it faced the bare, grimy windows.

'Except you'll be woken by that fuckin' great yellow ball that drops out of the sky each morning.' Smithy took over the controls of the spinning couch, dropping it back to its original position in the centre of our bare living room.

And so Jeff had moved in with as little impact and fuss possible. Five years later there is now no Jeff but his bed has not moved since the day he made us three. Before taking on the role of our lounge lizard, Jeff filled space at his parent's home until they turned his room into a TV room – which is sort of ironic as we'd done the reverse.

For the first few months Jeff trod as lightly around the place as some water bird across a pond of lily-pads for fear that he would send a ripple through our marsh. Before either Smithy or I would get up of a midday Jeff would have cleared his bedding, washed and dried a bunch of our T-shirts, cleaned some surface or stretch of flooring and been down the road to collect snacks with which to ensure our continued tolerance of him. He didn't know that we were as likely to bother to abandon him as we were of getting jobs and a mortgage. Finally, we woke one day to find a selection of pastries looking almost comfortable in our suddenly gleaming kitchen. Smithy nodded to me to hold Jeff down as he wrenched the clothes dryer off the bathroom wall and threw it over the balcony, onto the street. Next he stapled Jeff's doona and pillow to the couch and attempted the sacrificial burning of a croissant. Nothing was said during the exorcism, which sort of made it all the clearer, and for six months Smithy kept hold of Jeff's ATM card and only handed over cash for acceptable purchases.

Every so often Smithy would spring for the three of us and Maya to go to the movies with Jeff's money just so Jeff would feel comfortable that we were in some way indebted to him. His excitement at being our host never dulled when his pick of film failed to win a majority, his choice of refreshment was voted down, and his suggestion of seat row always seemed to be similarly vetoed.

Through the previews Smithy regularly slapped Jeff across the back of the head as he talked incessantly, which reminded us that at school Jeff was always placed next to the newly arrived Vietnamese kids so he couldn't converse easily.

When it first hit me that a pattern had formed of Jeff's every selection being somehow overridden I wondered if Jeff had ever sensed this as he never seemed to weary of coming up with ideas. There was never any agenda to block Jeff's choices and I was sure Smithy or Maya or Rat-Boy had no idea how many miss-hits he was accumulating.

Over the years I kept a mental record of Jeff's success with his choice for lunch option, video selection, beach destination, and while I grew to admire his resilience I looked forward to the day that this most minor of victories would be his. Only this flat-mate of ours – who Smithy had nicknamed 'Placid', which later morphed into 'Lake' and occasionally Domingo – could have maintained motivation in the face of such a poor win-loss record. Yet more often than you'd imagine, Jeff's opinion was sought on which girl, from a choice of two or more, Smithy should stay with. As soon as Jeff would offer Sonja, Smithy would settle on Alison.

Until Jeff realised a few years back that he was not just passing through our lives but was considered a permanent fixture, more valuable than any clothes dryer, he was the one who appeared to suffer most when the Sonjas and Alisons got the boot. It's a matter of learning what's detachable and what's not.

Washing and cleaning were not the way to score points within our flat – much better to collect lunch, pack cones, compile collections of *Simpsons'* episodes and sign up at the few video stores that don't have our address on their banned lists. Jeff continually proved handy in our dealings with local merchants. Just recently, for instance, Smithy had tried to sign up at the new Video Ezy in the plaza on the way back from the pub one night and was dismissed due to a lack of suitable ID. As Jeff and I waited outside we could hear Smithy threatening to ram a copy of *Gladiator* down the manager's throat and then leave after pulling a pivotal box from the base of a pyramid tower display of Coca Cola cases that sent the lot crashing to the ground. The next afternoon Smithy returned with Jeff, sending him in with only his Medicare card as we watched through the front window. Within a minute Jeff was signing a membership agreement. Just as he received bountiful portions at kebab shops and preferred treatment at Centrelink, so too had his demeanour won over Smithy's latest nemesis. When we joined Jeff inside the manager looked at Smithy, pointing: 'Hey, you're from before!'

Smithy just grinned at him as we each chose a video, Jeff's selection being ditched in a vote-off as we only had enough cash on us for two and a snack.

'Hey Lake, what do you want to eat?' Smithy called as he returned Jeff's choice of movie to the shelves.

'What about salt and vinegar chips?'

I thought it brave of Jeff to nominate not only snack type but also flavour; though I guess he had hedged somewhat by responding with a question rather than a direct request.

'Nah, let's get popcorn.' Smithy's response was predictable.

We left Jeff to deal with the exchange and out-side I mentioned to a clueless Smithy about how Jeff never seemed to be in the majority on even the smallest of decisions and choices. 'So you hadn't noticed?' I asked Smithy.

'Nope, but it reminds me of that chick from the club I went out with – all the shows she liked on TV used to end after their first season, movies she wanted to see closed before she got her act into gear, new products at the supermarket that she hooked into would be discontinued by the time she'd run out and whenever she bought a CD single she always pre-ferred the B tracks.'

After a pre-video spliff we spent the rest of the afternoon watching the two movies and polishing off the popcorn. Unsatiated we collected enough coins from under the cushions on Jeff's bed for a weekly hire and sent Video Ezy's latest member down to collect another couple of hours of entertainment.

'What about *The Matrix*?' Jeff ventured.

'Good call,' Smithy replied.

17.

'Incurable but not disfiguring disease, country estate manners, uplifting, reclaimed love, sweeping nineteenth-century saga – ' the PM paints the rest of us a picture for a novel by a new author.

'Have any of you read it yet?' Goat asks the publishing side of the table.

'It's a brick of a book – I only have about a centimetre to go. It's a bit Catherine Cookson meets Ros Pilcher, set in the Australian squattocracy, 800 pages or so – great value if we do it at $29.95,' the PM responds.

Goat looks thoughtful. ' "Lucinda Waterstreet" – I'm concerned it might dog if it's sitting on the bottom rows of the A to Z fiction walls. Howsabout we go "Lucinda Corbett" so she sits at eye level, between Cookson and Bryce Courtney?'

'Done.' This PM never rambles.

Maxine, looking out for her side of the table, asks, 'Is the author saleable – how old is she?'

'Not as old as you'd think.' This PM is always diplomatic.

Goat looks around the room. 'Title?'

I avoid his eyes and Maet whispers to me: 'There's a certain style of title that works with this type of book – you'll suss it out quickly.'

' "Soon Enough It Comes"?' Emma offers. Goat nods in support of his deputy.

' "The Wind, My Friend"?' Kurt suggests with a smirk on his sun-chapped lips.

Maxine takes a shot for our team. ' "Bitter Harvest"?'

'Okay – I'll run some past the author,' the PM concludes.

Goat asks Kurt how many his team will sell.

No prevaricating this time. '10K'.

'Item 3 – *Beauty Naturally*.'

Goat charges into it. 'This is a great package – loads of colour, large format, power author from the States who will visit on release. It really has a lot of stuff. A very accessible read.' This explanation of the book makes it sound suitable for a simpleton and Maet flicks me a quick facial expression of an illiterate in-bred.

Kurt has heard enough. '8K.'

Emma, caught short by the speed of item 3 is nudged awake by Goat.

'Item 4. The new Katz – working title, "The Violinist".'

'Have you read Rupert Katz?'

Goat is looking at me.

While risking my luck at high odds has got me

this far, instinctive caution has me respond: 'Not for ages.'

Maet gives me a look to say that he knows I'm faking but he's completely cool with it.

The publishing manager updates me. 'Very faux lit, more Joanne Harris meets Jane Austen than Salman Rushdie – pretentious in-the-countryside stuff, a touch of *Anna Karenina* with dashes of French provincial style.'

With the PM's succinct summaries I wonder if any of us need read the books at all.

She continues. 'Previous book, *The Autumn Bees*, was part of that wave of literary fiction with bees in the title that followed on from the craze for books on snow. We pubbed it just when bees became the new snow and it got a little lost in the confusion. Quite worthy stuff, though, and I reckon he'll get his audience back.'

'*Bees* was a bit fat for reading groups – more than two and a half centimetres thick and you've lost them,' Maxine says.

'Katz's books always have an interesting twist that most other authors fail to achieve.' Goat directs his comments to the new guy, the non-Katz reader. 'As John Le Carre says, "there are loads of stories around and *The Cat Sat on the Mat* is a fine story but for an excellent story you need *The Cat Sat on the Dog's Mat*".'

Emma, with a keen eye on her watch, says, 'So I'm putting "The Violinist" down for 50 thousand copies – he's hit that number before. Any problems with that?'

Silence.

'Next book – "Mango Days",' Emma moves us along.

'We're pretty sure we'll do our own jacket for Australia. The one the US publisher has designed is complete crap. This is very much Bridget Jones meets *Sex and the City*. Mangoes are very in. The new bees. Fresh LA author, possible tour, it's all good.'

The PM turns to the meeting's scribe. 'Emma, can we roll this one for a future meeting till I have confirmation on jacket and visit?'

'Item 6 – Other Business.'

Not sure if that is a name of a book or if there is in fact other business to be done I look at Maet, who points to the door as a group of more people in black enters the room.

'Editors,' Maet mouths silently.

I look along the line of visitors and my gaze stops dead on the only person in the room. The more I stare the more her face becomes impossible to ignore. She hasn't looked my way as far as I can tell, but anyway I'm trapped in the headlights and can't change my expression from stunned mullet.

'Anna.'

Maet has read my mind or at least my gob-smackedness.

As each editor takes their turn to talk about projects – ones they are negotiating, ones that may turn into books – my attention is pinned to one station. The rest is just static.

Anna watches her fellow editors as each mumbles about who-knows-what. I watch her as she stands by the door fidgeting with her notes and shifting her weight from one foot to the other. She's wearing a simple black dress that matches her dark eyes and straight shoulder-length hair.

Quick glances either side of Anna reveal that one of the editors next to her is scouting for someone to use as the person they'll eyeball during their presentation. The nervous presenter selects me so I have to pretend to be listening to him whilst not wanting to remove my focus from Anna. I do my best for a while but end up dumping the guy.

Finally Anna commences her presentation, which is about a new series of DIY interior design books she'd like K&D to publish. My vote, for what it's worth, is Yes, Yes, and Yes. She is nervous like the previous presenter and keeps her gaze on her notes, rarely looking at those sitting around the board-room table. Her voice is as soft as her smile and as I imagine her dark hair to be. Have I just met – well, spotted – a person who will be in my life forever? Is she the type of person who needs to be won at first impression, on first meeting, or does she take her time to love? If I love her now, will it last the distance?

Each time you meet a new person, it's like getting a free lottery ticket – an opportunity, slim for sure, but no ticket no chance. The major prizes, great loves, are rare but magnificent. There are supplementary prizes in the form of good friends, but most tickets can be thrown away. Normally, people bounce off each other on impact. Could this be the car and the trip?

And then she is gone again as the editors file out of the room.

The battle between Maxine, Goat, Kurt Cobain and the PM over, we all drift away from the board-room back to hutches and offices. I make a beeline for the bathroom, past Naomi on Reception who, in preparation for a particular courier who calls around eleven each morning, is brushing her hair, checking her smile and applying fresh lipstick. I plan to do the same. Except the lipstick bit.

18.

It isn't entirely true to say Smithy had also not worked since leaving school. A couple of years back Maya's brother-in-law (Sascha's now ex-husband) organised for Smithy to help him out during a busy period at one of the local chop shops. Smithy's job entailed assisting with the chopping – pulling apart cars that someone willing to pay $3000 can have reconstructed to look completely different. Early in Smithy's short career his workload increased as he covered for Sascha's husband who stayed at home to be with Sascha after the miscarriage of their first pregnancy. The money Smithy earned during this time was as much as we'd ever heard any Bankstown boy to be making, but the cash he received for the extra shifts always found its way back to Sascha.

A couple of months after Sascha's miscarriage Smithy, never ordinarily the type to organise social events outside our regular routine, one Thursday became bizarrely insistent that we invite Sascha and her husband along to the Sporting Club for the Chinese banquet.

The club's main features, other than pokies, were its auditorium-sized restaurant with probably a hundred round tables resting under as many Lazy Susans, and its waiting staff, all with the most proper English names written on their badges but little further use for the language.

Initially Sascha declined – she wasn't feeling up to it – but Smithy spent the day encouraging Maya to hound her into joining us. A defeated Sascha eventually agreed on the condition it wasn't a late one. To ensure she didn't back out Smithy said Jeff, he and I would walk via their flat to collect them.

After a pre-Chinese spliff the three of us sauntered off to fetch the others even though their home was in the opposite direction to the club. Smithy, saying little, lagged behind Jeff and me, his long legs allowing him to take in the air and scenery above us as he strolled down the centre of the streets. When we got to Sascha's place Smithy, predictably, had a jibe at her husband, asking him how things were at The Lake – his family all hailing from Lakemba.

The night's social convener next buzzed into Sascha's living room and offered to set the video to record her favourite show – *ER*. That done, to lift Sascha's spirits we all subscribed to a little of Smithy's uncharacteristic buoyancy as we trekked to the club.

Still in no apparent rush, Smithy stopped to peer into any parked car that took his interest as if he were planning to snatch one for a trip to the chop shop.

To the uninitiated or unfortunate Smithy ordinarily seems sullen and disinterested. Not that he feels superior. It's as if his personality, when switched on, consumes such a vast requirement of kilojoules it would be impossible for Smithy to be lit for extended periods without him wasting away. So it goes that mostly Smithy cruises, and only those most familiar with him can pick up on variations in his mood. But when Smithy *does* shift into gear there are few who could resist being caught in his net.

This night Smithy outdid himself – at the time I felt that after his barrage of chat and charisma he'd be spending the next few days on a glucose drip. You'd figure it to be his antidote to a long day of watching TV if it weren't for the fact all days were spent much the same way and only rarely did they conclude with a visit from Smithy, raconteur on blow.

Presiding as our host from mixed entrée through to fortune cookies he ditched a recent long spell of charm hibernation, and regaled the group with an incredibly detailed analysis of his thoughts on a hundred topics – mainly of a scientific and natural history kind, a series of jokes that varied greatly in quality, and a comprehensive list of his idiosyncratic dislikes. Such a display would make most people appear to be self-centred bores but with Smithy it was like soaking up the energy from a dazzling spacecraft that happened to land, against all odds, in our backward mid-west Idaho town, for the briefest of visits. In the presence of such a visitor you'd hardly carry on a conversation with the pig farmer next door. I think Sascha, who would have drifted home much earlier, presumed Smithy was on speed and at the very least had been distracted, if only for a few hours. But there had been no white lines preceding this supernova's performance and eventually the list of things Smithy would prefer never to come across expired: cooked carrots, long-haired cats, antique cars, card games, spearmint, crunchy peanut butter, the colour yellow, cane fur-niture, egg on pizza, running shoes, asparagus, fifty-cent pieces, the entire North Shore, unflavoured milk, classic hits radio, shellfish, TV ads, avocado, pigeons and seagulls, undercooked chips, cold drinks served in mugs, hot drinks served in glass, non-button mush-rooms, and finally velcro.

By the time we left the club it was approaching ten o'clock and Smithy's energy level had sagged. He farewelled Maya, Sascha and her husband merely with a quick joke, as if to prove he wasn't really any different and to ensure no one was comfortable that his only targets were yuppies, gays and trendies.

'Why do women wear make-up and perfume? Because they're ugly and they stink.'

Jeff and I followed Smithy home but as he went straight to bed, presumably to recharge his empty batteries, I packed a cone and Jeff settled in to watch that night's episode of *Getaway* which he'd recorded while we were out. Like the rest of us, Jeff had never been on a plane but somehow he never doubted that such opportunities were just around the corner. It always reminded me of how he'd often get up before us and dress for the beach when it was pouring outside, Smithy and I both in our beds presuming that the previous night's planned adventure would be off. Occasionally the sun would relent and make a belated appearance, joining Jeff in his optimism, and Smithy and I would tag along as well.

Too stoned to bother fast-forwarding through the ads and upcoming previews we saw that the evening's episode of *ER* featured one of the female doctors suffering a miscarriage. The next day Maya told us that Sascha was miffed as Smithy, normally technically proficient, had stuffed up her video and recorded the wrong station. It didn't seem to irk Smithy that everyone thought he'd fucked up – he and Sherlock knew better.

19.

Would Jeff have loved Anna? He'd have smiled at her immediately and, even if she was still not won over by Declan, she'd surely have seen the glow reflected upon me from being Jeff's mate.

The remnants of chocolate ice-cream have dulled my bedroom walls so that what the window offers each morning should seem brighter than it does.

Out the window is Anna somewhere. Apparently she has a boyfriend. Maet had quickly filled me in on that as Declan Zombie spent the rest of yesterday waiting in his hutch for her to come past. She never did. My third-ever email was some quote that Maet re-titled 'Anna' and had forwarded to me: *I've learned that you cannot make someone love you. All you can do is stalk them and hope they panic and give in*. This gave me little confidence.

Anna already has a boyfriend – I don't want her to think I'm the sort who'd cut another guy's grass. I don't want her to be the sort who dumps or cheats, even for me. Catch 22. I wouldn't join a club that'd have me for a member and all that.

If it weren't for Jeff I'd have never had the opportunity to meet her and he'll never meet her now. When Maet told me about her rich parents and privileged upbringing across several hemispheres and streams of time zones the notion of just six degrees of separation seemed unlikely. Just a week ago Anna and I would have failed miserably to make any connections via sixty degrees of separation, let alone six. We'd know none of the same people, we'd have been to none of the same places – even Kevin Bacon couldn't have helped. Only now had our planets come anywhere near each other and they might just keep going. Will she get to know Dec, or will she just pass Declan by? Could it be possible that she could care for either?

Declan is meant to commence the third morning of his short life while Dec lays flattened by the prospect of another day.

While I was surviving yesterday's marketing meeting Smithy had also been busy. He and Maya had taken a trip into the city where Smithy stole himself a couple of Mormons. As Maya recounted the story to me and Rat-Boy at the pub last night after the two Mormons had finally slumped under our table, they'd never stood a chance.

Oozing his rarely employed but devastatingly powerful charm, Smithy had set after the pair of short-sleeved Utah folk who'd looked his way on George Street as if he were a Mormon himself.

Smithy had been happy to accompany Maya into the city but, as always, refused to join her in visiting the place where Jeff left us. Not wanting to be reminded of Jeff's going he missed out on seeing Maya, her hands softly cradling her stomach, talking sweetly to her unborn baby about our lost mate.

By the time Maya returned, the fresh-faced Mormon college graduates who'd stupidly dared glance Smithy's way had been spellbound by his tales of a better life.

And so Smithy distracted Bud and Chip like Jeff had been distracted, and the Mormons lost these two recruits, liberated by a sea of VB, a haze of bong smoke and a litany of swearing and laughter, refusing to answer their pagers like a couple of homing pigeons who'd seen France and refused the call to return to miserable old England.

As Bud or Chip sleep it off on Jeff's couch, the other on the kitchen floor, I search my bed in the vain hope a cigarette has found its way out of the empty packet that is squashed into my pillow like an unnoticed complimentary chocolate. From memory Rat-Boy, who could never get enough cash together to buy a packet himself, purchased my last five durries off me for two bucks.

It takes all the energy I have to prop myself up on both elbows so I can check my face in the mirror on the far wall. A panda blinks at me. Black-ringed eyes. I bury my face in the cool of a just-flipped pillow and see Anna's dismissive expression on meeting me later today. Her eyes will glaze as she sums me up with one look like the market researchers at the mall who never feel the need to inquire about the spending patterns of four unemployed, under-achieving, grunge-attired dope-heads. Will she be able to relate to me on any level? Maybe someone like me once cleaned her pool or stole her father's car.

'Hey Dec, wake up and smell the grass.' Smithy bounds into my room and shoves a freshly lit joint into my mouth as I make out that I've just woken.

'Just to keep you in the loop, Declan, going for-ward drugs will only be served in the sitting room – albeit 24/7,' he says, taking the piss out of my newly acquired marketing speak that I assume I vomited over the gang last night.

As I smoke my breakfast-in-bed Maya calls in to announce that she is going to fix a nice greasy spread of bacon and fried eggs for Bud and Chip before we set them free. It's only fair that they decide their future path on full stomachs.

Jeff would have loved to be among all these people – he'd confided in me once that he loved sleeping in the living room as it was the centre of the house, the centre of the action (as limited as that generally was). To hear the trains at night, the hoons drag racing in the early hours of the morning, and to be surrounded by our noises at all times comforted him and reminded him that he was never alone, never the only one not asleep. No wonder he remained with us now, like a faithful dog at our heels.

I hear Bud or Chip request a side of hash browns. Maya, laughing, asks if they'd like fries with their meal. It seems that Smithy has done these guys a big favour by throwing a little chaos in their path. They chat excitedly to Maya as they scoff their fatty plate-loads and plan their big adventure – dumping their street jobs and hitching north. The irony is that they'll end up making us lot look pretty fucking boring.

Smithy leaves my room, assuming that I'll be blacking up for work, and I hear him farewelling the guys whom he has renamed Spud and Dip on account of their new lives.

Collecting my old jeans and a barely held-together T-shirt from the floor I slip easily into my previous life's, my real life's, attire. While Smithy and Maya wave Spud and Dip farewell from the balcony I, priorities in place, call K&D's number.

'Kyle & Deutsch, Naomi speaking.'

'Hi Naomi, its Declan.'

'Good, thank you.'

'Naomi – can you put me through to Maet please?'

'Sure.'

'Hey Maet – I'm not feeling too well so don't think I'll be in today.'

'Not lovesick are you?' Maet says and I can hear him grinning.

'No,' I say vaguely, unsure if it's true, 'just a bit out of sorts.'

'I can't hear any flight announcements so must be kosher,' Maet says bizarrely and my silence provides a question mark.

'It's just that once I called work from the airport to skive off for a long weekend in Noosa. Just as Maxine answered you could hear *This is the last call for flight QF19 to Darwin*.'

Taking no offence at the implication that I am skiving – as in fact I am – the thought occurs to me that it's pretty fucking lucky that Maet keeps surprising me with how easy-going a boss can be.

'Okay, buddy – see you tomorrow.' He lets me off the hook with no further need to explain.

This day is for the three of us – to build us, to hold us, to keep us. We'll do nothing together like it always was and hopefully can remain. To hold onto our nothing is the most important thing for me now and, while I'll be at work tomorrow, my future lies in today. I can have both lives – I'm not trading one for the other.

Smithy, Maya and I re-attach ourselves to The

Oasis for a few pre-kebab bevies and a couple of games of pinnie. Placing my three dollars into 'Elvira', Smithy, all-time pub champion on this machine, gives me his inside tip. 'If I can give you just one piece of advice about multi-ball it would be to focus your eyes at all times on your flippers.'

20.

Day four of work – three if you don't count yesterday.
Pretty soon the fuzz in my navel will be black.

Normally a harsh critic of my own looks, I note
that post-shower my hair has strangely fallen perfectly, my teeth appear white, eyes clear. If Anna is
not at work today then it'll be fate's determination.
As it's already eight-thirty I decide to take Smithy's
now unregistered car – that way I've got a greater
chance of preserving what the morning has dished up.

Even though I was the last to drive the car, my
mood, inspired by the luck I feel that Anna's first
sight of me may not be so disappointing, requires
me to adjust the rear-vision mirror upward as I sit
slouch-free. To maintain the buoyancy I ditch the
melancholy Nirvana CD that starts up when the car
reacts immediately to my instructions and tune the
radio to the station that serves dance and techno
for breakfast. A succession of green lights greets
Declander, supermodel for the day, and his mate's

clapped-out car that may well be on its last outing if the city's parking inspectors are not all slacking off.

Driving into the city obstruction free, I allow my mind to contemplate all the things that I'd have be: Anna, something more of Jeff than his credit card and sofa, and a way to have both Dec's world and Declan's. While not global peace or a rescue package for the ozone layer, my hopes for them ordinarily seem just as forlorn, so I make the most of this rare natural high and daydream the drive away.

From the five cars that I've allowed to pull in in front of me I've received four waves including a taxi-driver acknowledgement which represents one of the rarer of the species and therefore most valuable. The only blip is some old fart with Victorian number plates. On good days even a bank robber on the way to a job will flip you a wave if you let them ahead but no, not your crabby old geezers. Overall though, my wave strike rate further suggests that this is a morning rich in possibility.

I dump the car for the day in a two-hour parking spot a few blocks from the K&D offices and grab the CD player and discs in case it's towed before my return. If I'm not mistaken I score a look from two blonde secretary types as I stride confidently across the road and then a glance from a guy pulling into a parking station. While to some the latter represents half a point at best, I'm not complaining as the sheer force of such goodwill is my only hope of unbalancing the cool, detached Princess Anna.

The lift is full so I can't check if my good fortune has deserted me yet. It's Thursday, and people who share office space but little else are trying to force conversations initiated by a lame 'Not long till the weekend'. A smile, a wink and silence.

I linger as the lift empties completely on my floor and practise a winning grin in the mirrored back-wall. Naomi on Reception, busy photocopying pages from a pile of cookbooks left for perusal by a door-to-door salesman, surprises me by enquiring into my health. This disorients me momentarily – I was hoping that the look I'd cultivated was not one of illness – until I remember my day off and thank her for the concern. She flings me an oversized farewell card hidden inside an interoffice envelope and tells me to sign it there and then so she can pass it on to people as they arrive.

What if this, my best day, is Anna's last day? I quickly check the scribbled messages and am relieved to see some guy called Duane is calling it quits – though Naomi on Reception has wished him 'Happy Birthday!' A message from someone called Virginia simply says: 'Go Screw Yourself'.

Deciding not to waste today's opportunity on the off-chance that Anna will come by the publicity hutches while my look holds I take the card with me before Naomi on Reception has a chance to notice. I acknowledge Maet, his hair today a Beckham mohawk, on my way down the corridor and will myself on toward the clump of desks and barriers peopled by the editorial team, the 'seafood extender' of the publishing world as I'd heard Maxine refer to them on my first day.

Anna is sat at her desk and doesn't look up until I'm right beside her. *Smile, smile, smile* my mind implores my face. Eventually it does but with my luck I fear it may have appeared a little lop-sided. She smiles back briefly and breaks the silence with a straightforward, 'Can I help you?'

She has no idea who I am.

'Um, yeah, I'm Declan from publicity. Naomi on Reception asked me to pass this card on to you for signing,' I say as nonchalantly as I can.

'I've already signed it,' she whispers, opening the card and pointing out her name. 'I'm Anna.'

'Nice to meet you Anna.' I put out my hand to shake but she is already looking back at her screen.

'Okay – I'll keep it going around,' I say weakly and dump the card on the guy's desk opposite hers.

As I beat a hasty retreat out of seafood extender territory I see Anna jump from her chair and retrieve the card from her neighbour, who is wearing a shirt styled on those red, white and blue vertically-striped laundry bags. 'Sorry Duane, you don't need to sign this one.'

I return humiliated to my safety zone with Maet and the Naomis. Feeling more familiar with what's expected of me, the rest of the day passes reasonably smoothly. Though occasionally my mind ventures back to my earlier faux pas with Anna and I sink a little more. Naomi A, her bare skull shining under the fluorescent lighting, takes me through the process of allocating the proof copies of my first assigned book – the upcoming chick-lit title, *Mango Days*. In what seems a pretty random manner she highlights names within a vast database of reviewers, editors, presenters and producers and then prints off address labels. The jacket design for the Australian printing of the book has still to be decided so the proof copies have a plain card jacket with my contact details. I decide to reserve a copy to read and as a memento.

As the author of *Mango Days* will be touring in a few months, Maet asks me to observe as he finalises plans for a tour he's been organising for a book on US talk shows. *Written by the new American voice of pop culture this book takes a humorous behind the scenes look at the phenomenon of Rikki Lake, Jerry Springer and others.* Or so Maet's spiel goes. After an hour his pitch has become embedded in my short-term memory – he's now recounted it to radio producer number twenty in an attempt to line up an itinerary packed full of live interviews that will supplement the book launch he's organised at a store in the city. Maet assures me that the author is not high-profile enough yet to score a gig on TV. It sounds pretty interesting though, so I grab a copy of the proof of this book as well.

My steep learning curve is not without the occasional plummet. A magazine editor calls to request contact details for an author I've never heard of but whom the caller assures me K&D has published for years. Determined to be self sufficient for once, I track the author's contact details on the database and call back the magazine editor, passing on phone numbers and an email address. Given the closeness of our working space – several times people I'm speaking to on the phone have thought we had a crossed line – I'm aware that Maet and the Naomis are listening as I handle the enquiry. In my attempt to impress them with my initiative I put on the most professional voice I can muster. Only when I've hung up do all three of my comrades raise their heads in unison above our flimsy low hutch walls, Maet being allowed the honour of informing me that the author has been dead for two years.

I suspect the three office Naomis share more than just their name when Naomi on Reception buzzes me via the intercom with 'Declan, call from a Bill Shakespeare on line two.'

Calls from beyond the grave continue through

the afternoon until Naomi on Reception announces Alex Smith of Vanderlay Industries.

'Hey, Smithy.'

'Me and Maya are out the front with a coupla of post-work spliffs for ya – nice fat fuckers they are too.'

I grab my proof copies and the CD player and discs, cop one last crack from Maet about publicity opportunities for authors who've carked it, and leave my good hair day and all its false promise of a break-through with Anna behind.

We find an empty pier down at the nearby wharves where Smithy and I share the first spliff, the three of us leaning against the same massive pylon, each observing different worlds. My eyes blur from the inside as I smoke the second joint alone – my reward for working a full day. Slowly my head gives in to the dope's sweet lilt as Maya starts on *Mango Days*, and Smithy laughs intermittently as he fossicks for gems in the book that parodies US talk shows.

I wake when the sun finally calls lights out, and with the extinguishing of their reading lamp, Smithy and Maya get me to my feet so we can find a drink.

The closest pub is not too bad even though a band is threatening to start up. When I return with the beers and Coke, Smithy is telling Maya the story of Maisie's dog, Silk, and how Maisie immortalised him just before he died by trotting him across the wet cement outside her house. This is not the first time Smithy has talked around the idea of creating something that celebrates Jeff alive rather than heralding him dead. Maya, resting her drink on her massive stomach, tries to pacify him: 'But we'll always have our memories of Jeff.'

'Fuck that, I want something concrete.'

Changing the topic slightly I toast the fact that we were given a chance to know Jeff better than anyone else. Completely changing the topic Maya follows on with a toast to the fact that we all have our eyesight. Smithy goes next, swigging thanks that we weren't born on the North Shore, and by the time our gratitude for all the things we normally take for granted has been expressed I'm completely wasted. Unfortunately the band has started and we're asked to leave shortly after Smithy calls out to the woeful lead singer, 'Shame that's a microphone mate and not a fuckin' magic wand.'

After verifying that the Passat has been towed for good Smithy and I stumble behind Maya to the train station. Once aboard our very own carriage I decide to update my two best friends on Anna and Maet, without letting on that I would have these two colleagues complete my full hand if I could.

Maya asks Smithy the question I never could – 'What do you think of the new Dec – this Declan guy?' – she smiles at me, acknowledging she knows that I've been dying for Smithy's take on all of this.

Smithy looks at us both in turn and says, 'Forever there has just been the Cherry Ripe bar – we've never wanted or imagined any different. Then one day you wake up and without any fanfare there's the fucking Strawberry Ripe. How come we never thought of that?'

I'm too off my face to have a clue what that means, and plan to ponder it when my brain stops shedding cells at an accelerated rate. But I think it sounds positive.

21.

In the three weeks since Anna first dismissed me I have kept a mental record of the times our paths have crossed, eagerly trying to read favourable connotations into moments she's most likely discarded like superfluous words in her latest manuscript. All put together they might appear to amount to something but on their own barely provide the flimsiest of circumstantial evidence of interest. Most mornings now I run through the list of highlights in order to convince myself that there is a chance for Anna and Declan, and maybe, though even more unlikely, for Anna and Dec.

The star moment of two weeks ago was Duane's farewell drinks where Anna, given a choice of three empty chairs around the boardroom table, chose the one that while not actually next to me, was by any measure closer to me than the other two.

I've registered last week's highlight as the first instance of Anna actually referring to me by name. Admittedly it was merely to ask me to move a box of proof copies that was blocking the passageway by the publicity hutches, but she could have asked Maet or one of the Naomis and her instinct was to choose me. The fact that Maet is senior and the Naomis female does not diminish the merit of the moment as K&D is a fervently non-discriminatory workplace.

And so far this week I'm selecting yesterday's marketing meeting, when I'm sure Anna had me in her peripheral vision for several stints. To test this, without warning I sprung a sudden look at the ceiling – and noted that Anna had followed suit.

Most days, of course, all the above seems massively outweighed by certain facts. She has a boyfriend, comes from a wealthy family and normally is completely oblivious to my existence.

Yet the heightened sense of excited insecurity that comes from being torn by love diminishes as time eats away. Last night, drinking and playing pool at the pub, spending some of my first-ever pay, I reckon two hours passed before I remembered to think again of Anna. Nothing in my life outside of K&D reminds me of her, just as nothing in my life as Declan from Publicity brings my dead mate easily to mind.

Ever since I told Smithy and Maya about Anna they've hounded me daily about progress and my flimsy highlights disappoint them. Smithy, out of frustration, has set me a target of asking Anna for a drink before our current bottle of shampoo runs out.

From the moment Smithy's mother picked him a younger brother from the street he has set me goals that involve accomplishing something against a time clock that bears no relevance to the task itself. From eating all non-meat items on your dinner plate before an ad break finishes to reading a chapter of a book before he can pack and smoke a full cone, the games have generally involved some form of self-improvement. Not surprisingly, Smithy is now washing his short hair daily while I'm making do with five drops of shampoo every other day. I could of course reject the challenge, but with Smithy that never really seems an option. Better to try to slow the procedure or redefine the conditions. My protest that Anna already has a boyfriend who happens to be in a wheelchair and asking her out might define me as a cad scored no alterations to the terms of the task, Smithy arguing that she won't know that I know she has a partner. It is up to her to decide if that relationship is going to continue or not: Smithy has clarified the rules of dating as he sees them.

From the moment I get off the train I commence my familiar internal chant. *Don't be so intense around Anna, don't be so intense around Anna.* That done I imagine how a coolly confident Declan might deal with possible Anna interactions. I take a pause from my racing mind and walk the rest of the way to Universal Tower with the Discman I've borrowed from

Sascha tuned into an upbeat, funky station so that I'll be geed-up just in case. Pathetically I realise that for the first time I can recall I'm really listening to the words of a song. Just missing a lift, I gaze into the stainless steel doors. They offer a hazy view at best but, as I try to make out my reflection a familiar figure arrives clear as day in the scratchy silver, standing beside me.

Deciding to play it cool, I remain looking ahead but in case Anna plans to acknowledge me I discreetly turn the volume of my Discman to silence. To my bewilderment I can hear Anna's distinctive voice singing softly to the very same song. Peering again into the cool doors just as they open I see thin leads running out of her ears. How can I show her that we've been listening to the same music? That we may have more than nothing in common?

In my rush to increase the volume on my Discman I somehow unleash it from my waist, sending it crashing to the floor of the lift. The top springs open to reveal a Green Day CD, which Anna will be looking down at as I clumsily scoop up the player from among at least eight pairs of feet. Naturally, after I've stood back up, each pair of feet elects to get off at a different floor and so I take the longest ride of my life watching the numbers on the display panel and listening to Anna sing solo.

Following Anna off at our floor I slip into the

K&D unisex bathroom to check how I looked, other than dunderheadish, when Anna saw me. In the same mirror that has reflected her beautiful face I concede that, despite lank hair, things could have been worse. At least my teeth are clean. The very game engineered to get me to know Anna may just ruin my chances – maybe I'll grab some shampoo at lunchtime and wash my hair here at work. I probably won't, though, as the rules of Smithy's challenge are quite clear.

It feels like a full day already and it's barely nine o'clock.

'Hey Greaseball!' Maet greets me as I saunter into the publicity zone.

'Hey,' I say to the guy, who today is underneath a fortress of spiked hair.

'Do you want to help me finalise the itinerary for the talk-show book?' Maet says brightly, picking up on my despondency.

I decide to show some interest. 'Sure – when does the author arrive?'

'Monday. Book launch Tuesday, radio interviews Wednesday and Thursday, goes back Friday.' Maet has worked on the tour for a full month, but he summarises it as if it has been a snap.

'Have you had a read of it?' Maet enquires.

'Not yet, but my flatmate has and he pissed himself,' I respond, without the aid of accepted publishing lingo.

'How long have you guys lived together?' Maet asks.

'Since I was eight,' I reply, knowing further elaboration will be necessary. 'Smithy's sort of like my brother actually. Long story.'

'It's quite a hike to commute each day – think you'll stay in Bankstown?'

'Maybe not – wouldn't mind trying somewhere different,' I declare, surprising myself.

'Well, if you want to check out the inner west you should come over to my place one night. We can grab a few beers.'

'Cool.'

Maxine joins us. 'All okay for next week's tour?'

'No worries,' Maet confirms.

Checking my emails in the vain hope that Anna has been overcome by the need to write to me I click open an invitation from someone called Guy Murdoch inviting me and a bunch of others to 'supper' at his house in Neutral Bay.

'Who's Guy Murdoch?' I call over my partition, forgetting Maxine is still in our zone.

Maet leans over the half-wall and mouths 'Goat' so only I can see as Maxine says none too subtly: 'The Marketing Manager – you know – weird yellowish eyes and hands as cold as airline cutlery.'

I smile knowingly, not wanting Maxine to jig I've never been on a plane. After all, I've worked in the book industry in the States.

'Are you going?' Maet asks Maxine, diverting further discussion about in-flight utensils.

'I replied that I'll need to check with Sebastian first,' Maxine announces as she strides back to her office.

I can tell Maet has no idea who the fuck Sebastian is.

Maet suggests we grab some sandwiches from the foyer cafeteria so I ditch any lingering notion of spending my lunch break washing my hair. As we head toward the takeaway counter Maet nudges me, directing my eyes to a table nearby. Anna and Goat's assistant Emma are perusing the eat-in menu, discussing the foccacia options.

Emma deliberates out loud between turkey/cranberry and chicken/avocado.

'They all sound good to me except ham/asparagus – my two most hated foods together!' Anna declares with a wince.

After we quietly order our sandwiches Maet loiters with me by the counter so I can continue to listen to Anna and Emma's conversation.

They chat on about Emma's upcoming overseas trip after telling the waitress that they are waiting for someone to join them before ordering. Maet and I pay for our sandwiches as slowly as possible to stretch out my opportunity for eavesdropping. As we finally turn to leave we see a guy in a wheelchair join their table. Now, no prompting from Maet can unfreeze me.

Eventually Emma spots us and waves to come and say hello. I follow Maet to the table where Emma introduces us to Anna's boyfriend, who is grumpily scouring the menu as Anna tries to elicit a friendly greeting from him. With nothing much to say, Maet and I offer our goodbyes.

The waitress returns to the table and Anna's boyfriend orders himself a foccacia of ham and asparagus.

22.

'Strange name that – Maet.'

'I think my mother chose it to shit my father. Apparently it was a typo she made at work when she was pregnant with me – and instantly liked the look of it. But I stuck with it rather than the name my father gave me.'

'Your parents called you different names?' I ask, incredulous.

'I can't recall them agreeing on anything much,' Maet says.

'So what did your father call you?'

Maet looks at me with a smile. 'Lance.'

'Good you had a choice, then.'

Maet and I are on our third beers at his local in Erskineville. Though not as dingy as The Oasis it's not the world away that I'd imagined. The derros and the unfashionable bar staff help to make me feel comfortable, as does the fact many of the punters stagger on arrival not just departure. I try to remember the last time I've gone boozing without Smithy but come up with nothing.

My assimilation tour of Sydney's inner west, guided by Maet, is to comprise drinking in a couple of the pubs in Erko, followed by some food from one of the myriad of Thai restaurants on King Street.

'So your parents taught you duplicity from an early age?'

I construct a sentence that I reckon has never seen the light of day in my usual haunts. Frankly I'm still a little intimidated, and without Smithy to set the conversation tone I decide to go upmarket so as not to appear what I am.

'I guess – but mostly they aimed to instill small-mindedness,' Maet says.

'Whaddya mean?'

'Well, like when I was eighteen and I told them that I was gay so they made an appointment for me to see a psychologist.'

Maet slips in the fact that he is gay as if he expected I'd know. I try not to look surprised and imagine how I'm meant to react, how Smithy would react, I guess. 'Vagina decliners' he calls them. But maybe I don't know what Smithy would do. It amazes me that Maet presumes I'll be cool with it – I don't think he realises the gulf that exists between my world and what I imagine his to be. Suddenly I feel less than completely sure ours is the only way.

'So did you go to the shrink?' I ask as nonchalantly as I can muster.

Maet grins. 'When I told the psychologist that my parents had sent me to see her because I was gay she sent me home with an appointment card for them.'

I laugh at his parents and at myself.

Maet looks at me intensely and says, 'Can I ask you a personal question?'

Shit. Fuck. 'Yeah, I guess,' I stammer.

'When are you going to wash your hair?'

Fuck I'm an idiot.

I explain to Maet about Smithy and his task-setting, especially the connection between my lifeless hair and Anna.

'So you really like her then?'

'Uh-huh.'

Maet rubs it in. 'What's your next move ... or first move?'

'She has a boyfriend – you saw him – he's in a wheelchair.'

'What I saw was a petulant prat.'

'If she were my girlfriend I'd be fucking happy the whole time – how could you be so sullen alongside her?' I declare, making an enemy of the wastrel she's spending her days with. 'Only catch is, I'm completely fucking stupid and pathetic whenever she's within twenty metres of me. I forget what's regular to say and do – it's like she somehow demagnetises my normality fields and it's all I can do to recall how to walk in a straight line and comprehend basic sentences. I feel my face contorting into expressions there aren't even names for.'

Maet responds by asking how I've ever managed to get a girlfriend in the past. I realise the irony of a gay guy advising me on how to approach a girl and hope, if the tables are ever turned and Maet seeks my thoughts on how to improve his love life, I'll be as un-homophobic as Maet is un-heterophobic. But he'd probably be wise not to waste his time – I'd struggle to relationship-manage a pair of randy rabbits.

'So what is the difference between Lia and Anna?' Maet asks after I've given him a brief rundown on my only long-term relationship.

'With Lia it was easy as I only got to really like her after we were already together and everything else was stable. It was nice, like being cool in summer – whereas Anna could be warmth in winter but I don't reckon I can get the flame going. Am I making sense?'

Two pubs done, we walk along King Street checking out the vibe in the restaurants: Thai Foon, Thai Land, Thai Riffic, Thai Tanic. From the identical menus with identical prices we choose one as good as any.

From Moneybags to Pad Thai, I find myself telling Maet about my life till now. The beers I've had suggest to me that it is okay to reveal to my workmate that I've not worked since school, barely been out of Bankstown and have spent the last fifteen years shrinking my brain with drugs and beer.

I ponder aloud whether my friendship with Smithy is conditional on smoking dope, hanging together day in and out, and having no money or plans. Funny thing is that Maet, who for me represents the opposite of life till now, seems to envy my simple life and as hard as I try I can't detect any patronising tone.

'I think you under-rate Smithy,' he says. 'I bet he's glad that you're venturing out of your comfort zone. He sounds pretty smart to me and wouldn't discard his best mate just because you have a job and want to discover different people, different places.'

So Maet sticks up for Smithy. I doubt Smithy would do the same for him. Weird.

Maet makes it sounds like I've planned a great adventure, daring to go where no one from my tribe has gone before. Truth is, I just wasn't tied down fast enough when the wind came along.

'Don't you like pineapple?' Maet asks as I start on the red duck curry.

'Love it,' I reply, confused.

'You're joking – you look like you've eaten a mouthful of sand.'

How can it be that my facial expressions don't match my emotions? How long has this been going on?

'I thought I was emitting a satisfied glow,' I say, awaiting Maet's interpretation.

'It was a cringe. You'd best not order anything you love if you do get to go on a date with Anna.'

'I doubt she'd ever go out with someone like me,' I whine.

Maet grabs a wedge of lemon from the plate of salt and pepper calamari and shoves it in my mouth. 'Suck on this.'

'Sour,' I say defining my expression, hoping for a match.

Maet confirms my worst fears. 'Sweet.'

We decide the situation is not irreparable: if I manage to gather the resolve to ask Anna out then I'll wash my hair properly and spend some time fine-tuning my facial expressions in front of a mirror. It might be as simple as grimacing when I'm happy and grinning when I'm not.

We are the last to leave the restaurant so get an especially warm farewell from the tired staff. As we make our way back to Erko and a different pub – The Imperial – I continue to rave on about Smithy, Anna and Jeff, stopping briefly to point out the witty street graffiti. 'Shut Up and Shop'. 'Do plastic things make it all okay?' Maet is less impressed by it.

The Imperial turns out to be a gay pub. I presume the reason Maet hasn't bothered to check if I'm comfortable with being here is that my face is dis-playing awkward as relaxed. There are two pool tables, a cavern of pokies and few women – just like The Oasis. I try to avoid eye contact with anyone, but soon realise I'm being pathetic as it's no more likely that a particular guy would like me than a particular girl and generally a particular girl doesn't.

'Are you going out with anyone at the moment?' I ask Maet, choosing not to use the word 'boyfriend' at this point. I've decided that I should show some interest in Maet's life given he has listened the whole night to my stories and dilemmas.

'No, single and horny,' he replies honestly.

'What sort of person do you like?' I ask steadfastly avoiding gender terms so as to avoid the onset of more stammering.

'He has to be a bloke, not a mincing queen, strong personality, sense of humour – a man's man.'

'And looks?' I continue, scanning the crowd for the first time as if I'm somehow going to help him find a match but instead discovering I'm the only person in the place with a shirt that's got a collar. Suddenly I'm the formal one.

'Blond and solid.'

For the briefest of moments I feel the weirdness of being peeved that a mate fancies a type other than my own. As luck would have it, my face reports this emotion with unprecedented accuracy.

'No offence Declan – at least I fancy your gender! It's just that opposites attract. In fact, you heteros take it further by liking people of the completely opposite sex.'

'I never thought of it that way,' I reply.

Maet decides to take the piss. 'You may not be my regular type but I've noticed a few eyes looking your way since we arrived.'

'I've a suspicion that even Excalibur could easily get picked up in this place.'

'Don't be so down on yourself. There's a confidence-building element to turning any head, and girls generally don't leer at a guy unless he looks like Brad Pitt. Enjoy the attention.'

'Thanks Maet, but I reckon I'll stay on the straight and narrow.'

Maet easily outwits me. 'No worries, Declan. You can be straight with me.'

Before the candid conversation is over Maet has divulged that he lost his straight virginity at eighteen, and gay virginity at twenty, but hadn't slept with anyone sober until he was twenty-five.

We decide to play a game of pool and I tell Maet how Jeff used to drive Smithy nuts by sinking the black ball early in the game so that a remaining ball had to be reclassified as the black.

'Maybe you could have a pool table at The Oasis officially named as the Jeff Acton Table,' Maet suggests.

'Not bad, but I think Smithy wants to create a memorial that might ordinarily be reserved for those whom society deems superior to people like Smithy, Jeff and me. A pool table in our dingy local wouldn't say enough.'

'Well, what about one of those park benches? I've seen ones dedicated to politicians, writers, actors.' Maet's interest is genuine.

'Park bench is good. Jeff did like to lay around a lot, especially on grass. But that's the thing – memorials reserved for famous people are reserved for famous people only.'

'Let me think about it some more.' Maet gives a wink, and sinks the black so small red is the new black.

'Thanks for the advice about Smithy, Anna and Jeff. You got anything, other than finding something blond and solid, that I can help with?' I ask sincerely. But what advice could I give someone like Maet?

He laughs and says, 'If you see my place you'll know what I need – a huge skip and the willpower to fill it with the crap that I've collected over the years. I envy you for owning so little stuff. It must make life so less complicated.'

'Can't you just stop buying things?'

'It sounds easy but it's not.' Maet sinks the small red with at least four more of his balls still on the table. 'I can't go cold turkey.'

I smile and sink small green to win the game. 'Let me think about it some more.'

Maet waits with me at Erskineville Station till the last train arrives in case I doze off and miss it. 'See ya tomorrow mate,' I call from my window as the train lurches off.

'See ya, Declan.'

'It's Dec. Call me Dec.'

23.

'Smithy told me last night about some town in Germany where each Tuesday anyone who wants to get rid of stuff that's likely to be wanted by others puts it out the front of their house. People then cruise around all night picking up furniture or whatever they need. Anything not gone by the morning has to be taken back in.'

But Maet's an addict. 'Problem is I'd be picking up more each week than I'd be putting out.'

If Maet really does want to help us create a fitting tribute to Jeff then I wanted to repay the favour by taking his problem seriously. I've spent most of the morning working on a few helpful guidelines in preparation for our first coffee break of the day.

'Smithy is the most minimalist person I know – our flat is so bare that it permanently looks as though we've just been robbed. If the landlord ever sends a tradesman over to fix something I always make out that we've just moved in. Smithy told me once that the smell of shopping turns his stomach. I don't think it helps that he has no money but I doubt he's pur-chased anything non-perishable for more than a year.'

As I offer these pearls I worry again that the gulf between my two friends might be impossible to bridge. But I soldier on. 'I've prepared a few guidelines for our two-pronged attack on your situation. I call it 'Reduction and Restriction'. First up we reduce the crap you've got, then we set up rules that restrict what you can buy or collect from now on.'

Maet looks seriously impressed that I've gone to so much bother, even if it was during time I was meant to be working. I hand him a copy of what I've come up with, including a few motivational quotes I found on the net: one from Walt Whitman about how cool it would be to be an animal as they're not made demented by the pursuit of possessions and another from some dude called William Morris who says you should have nothing in your houses that you do not know to be useful, or believe to be beautiful.

The first level in the reduction stage is to question anything that has the sole purpose of holding some-thing else. I explain to Maet that he'll need to be thorough and completely honest in how he measures whether any item is really necessary.

'Borrowing again from Smithy I've decided to set you the following goal – for every "holder" item that you keep then you must throw out another.'

And so in exchange for keeping his bed – which

after all is just a mattress holder – Maet sacrifices his battery rack, a storage device that keeps your like-sized batteries sorted together. To enable him to keep food-holding devices like plates, bowls and glasses – though the number of each is to be reduced to match the number of chairs he has in his house – Maet gives up his decorative telephone-book covers, toilet-roll holder and TV cabinet.

As we progress through the inventory of Maet's household possessions the cuts become deeper and coffee becomes lunch.

'Level two of reduction involves all other items, with the rule of thumb being that if you have not worn it, listened to it or watched it in the last year then out it goes – except for things you genuinely treasure.'

'So I can keep gifts?' Maet tries to claw back some ground.

'Only if you truly love the person who gave it to you. Better a crap present from someone you care for than a passable item from someone you never think about.'

With reduction plans in place I next address the restriction phase.

'Other than food, toiletries and the like the only items you can buy for the next year are clothes, books and CDs. Definitely no furniture, appliances or knick-knacks. With clothes you can only buy something when you've thrown out another piece. The aim is to wear out the stuff you've already got. You can only buy a new book when you've completed reading one, and as for CDs – well, you can't really have too many CDs.'

Maet, by now, is flabbergasted by my efforts, but kindly avoids any comparison to my less sophisticated approach to my job. Somehow I've survived a bunch of weeks at Kyle & Deutsch doing little more than following directions from Maet and the Naomis with very little creative input on my behalf. Work-wise it's pretty clear Maet knows that I have no idea what I'm doing but has decided that he isn't going to blow me out of the water, even to the point of supporting the few hare-brained ideas I've floated when pressured to contribute at a marketing meeting (reminding me of how Smithy never contradicted Jeff in front of anyone other than Maya or me). Just maybe by the time others outside the department cotton on to my greenness I'll have the experience I said I had. The confidence I've never had.

After helping Maet construct his final itinerary to send off to the US author, who arrives on Monday, we grab all the Naomis we can find and start Friday night drinks early. The lame but convenient venue is generally mocked by the staff of K&D, who represent an amazing range of Sydney tribes. Designed to catch city workers on their way elsewhere, the only feature the bar hangs its hat on is its location nestled among a crop of towering office buildings.

So it is that weekend surfers, yuppies, suburbanites, feminists, anarchists, marrieds, gays, ferals, cowboys, westies, expats, greasers, sports hooligans, goths, nerds, hippies, bikers and at least one slacker commence the shedding of their weekday personas in a haze of cigarette smoke that for the first time in the week has been liberated from the footpaths and building entrances of the city streets.

Conversation mostly centres on absent co-workers, so my interest levels remain dormant until Anna's name is mentioned. A fleeting comment by Naomi on Reception about how obnoxious Anna's boyfriend is when he comes into her foyer causes me to come so to life that my bar stool takes a small jump. On my behalf Maet attempts to get Naomi on Reception to reveal more inside Anna information but she's quickly onto the well-worn topic of the eleven o'clock courier whom she declares, between gulps of her pina colada, can 'deliver his package to me whenever he wants'.

Slowly, in the hours between afternoon and night, the three Naomis form an increasingly tighter huddle. Maet and I get back to the issue of his grand attack on materialism. I attempt to bolster Maet's resolve to start relocating his unnecessarys onto the street when he gets home lest the inspiration wanes in the light of day. Deridingly I tell stories of couples spending their weekends at the mall compiling their bridal registries, street people who have no home but still worship the meagre possessions they collect in shopping trolleys and carrier bags, and housewives who crowd onto buses for tours of factory outlets in the name of a social outing.

I'm pretty sure why I'm so keen to see Maet place the things he really doesn't want or need on the street for others to collect and cherish but I present a more logical argument.

'Think of the fewer things you'll have to clean, fix, move, arrange, replace, insure, store.'

Maet leaves me on the street corner outside the bar as he heads off to the train station and I wait for Smithy and Maya to collect me in a car Smithy has borrowed for the weekend. Sat on a fire hydrant I watch others ignore me until my time and place happily meet with those who want me.

24.

Two o'clock and so far today all I've consumed is one cone, a shared spliff and three beers. It being pointless to watch *Jerry Springer* alone, Saturday has become reserved for journeying through the previous week's episodes that Smithy records while I'm at work.

As the studio audience chants 'Jerry, Jerry, Jerry ...' neither of us can be bothered to venture out for food. By the time five hours have stung our blurring eyes it's as if the past week has been shared as it always was. I wonder if Smithy ever feels as if I've abandoned him but decide it's okay to mention my other life so that maybe he can share in it.

'They're having an international day at work next week – we're all s'posed to bring some food from our native culture for everyone to share – whaddya reckon?' I ask as Jerry's wrap-up comments come to an end.

'Chicken nuggets.'

Although I'm keen to find out if Maet has taken the

plunge and offloaded some excess stuff onto the kerb outside his house I dismiss thoughts of taking Smithy's borrowed car and driving past. I'm stoned and, anyway, weekends need to remain here just a while longer.

Come Monday morning I shift effortlessly into Declan mode as soon as I alight from the Bankstown–City train. The rest of the publicity team is already on the phones as I slip into my box. Impatient for news from Maet I keep glancing over the partition that divides us but he doesn't even look up and all the while his expression changes from rabbit in his hutch to rabbit in the spotlight. Whoever is on his phone is obviously not making his day.

'Coffee?' Maet's finally free but his expression has worsened. I think the bunny's been hit.

Some fellow K&D people share our lift and Maet signals me that he can't speak. Not until we've taken a table far from anyone who vaguely looks like they might be associated with publishing does he say anything.

'Jonson Weaver's not coming.'

'Who's Jonson Weaver?'

'The author of *Jerry, Rikki and Other Friends*. He's meant to arrive from the US today and start the tour tomorrow. I'm completely fucked.'

'What happened to him?'

'I left it to his agent to book the flights and it seems she never got round to it.' Maet downs his espresso in one gulp.

'Well that's not your fault then,' I declare optimistically.

'Thanks but it's totally down to me – I should have booked the flights myself or at least confirmed that the agent had done it. Fuck! Fuck! Fuck!'

'What's Maxine going to say?'

'She has a choice between telling me I'm slack or sacked.'

I contemplate the notion of trying to survive in my job without Maet ignoring my ineptitude. And though I feel selfish for thinking about my own skin when Maet looks so desperate I can't shake the picture of returning to Dec's world. Dec's world sans Jeff. Someone else's world.

'Surely firing you would be a little over the top?' I ask hopefully.

'Don't bet on it – you haven't been here long enough, dude. Maxine is totally insecure about her own position and may decide to take the opportunity to knock out the perceived competition when she gets the chance.'

I don't know what to say. What would Smithy do?

Maet continues to muse aloud. 'I'm going to have to cancel tomorrow night's launch and all the radio interviews lined up for the week.'

Something in my pants starts to vibrate and at first I try to ignore it until my brain can work out what's happening.

'I think your phone is ringing, Dec.'

I pull the nervy object from my pocket and recognise the flat's phone number on the screen. A blank look toward Maet is all that is needed for him to lean over and press the miniscule button that will allow me to talk to my home.

'What took so fucking long?' Smithy initiates my first ever discussion via a chocolate biscuit.

'Sorry – what's happening?'

'Not much – might go to the pub later with Maya. I'll set the vid to record our faves.' Smithy explains his Monday schedule.

'Thought I might cruise by and collect ya'all after work has done gone,' he continues, employing his credible, occasional Yank speak.

'Cool – I'll be out the front at five.'

I pass the phone to Maet for him to do whatever is necessary to end the call, but in the meantime Smithy's interruption has given me my first truly creative publicity idea.

'So Maet, let me get this straight. This is the guy's first book?'

'Yep.'

'Is his picture on the book?'

'Nope.'

'So nobody here has actually seen him before?'

'Nah.'

'D'ya think Smithy could be Weaver?'

Maet looks at me like I've spoken to him in Icelandic. 'Huh?'

'What if Smithy pretends to be this Jonson Weaver dude – does the launch and the radio interviews?'

A bit clearer but still foreign – possibly Finnish.

'Nobody here has seen this author and unless the tour reaches Bankstown no one will recognise Smithy. He's seen hundreds of these shows, he's read the book, he can do American accents and best of all he can bullshit like there's no tomorrow. What's more Smithy would do it – he's got absolutely nothing to lose.' I try not to sound too triumphant.

Seconds tick, then Maet finally responds. 'Yeah, but I'll lose my job if he stuffs up or if someone finds out.'

Silently I applaud myself that Maet is at least considering the idea and contemplate the coup of having someone like Smithy rescue someone like Maet. Could my old world have the power to save my new world? 'Sounds like you could lose your job if you don't come up with something,' I say, trying to make my far-fetched suggestion sound like a reasonable alternative to taking a chance with the disastrous truth.

'Do you really think Smithy could pull it off?' Maet asks wistfully.

Now that the plan is being seriously considered my confidence starts to waiver but I forge on regardless, as much for Maet's sake as my own.

'Sure – one of Naomi B's MBS authors is having a launch tonight. We can take Smithy along to that so he sees how they work. Then I'll get him to study Weaver's bio notes before you do the radio interviews Wednesday and Thursday.'

For the first time Maet is looking at me to take the lead and I'm a little freaked by the feeling that, like a vampire sucking in new recruits, I'll be responsible for introducing Maet to a full-blown scam.

'Let's do it!' Maet says a little too confidently.

Smithy has no idea what's in store as I wait outside Universal Tower for him to collect me for a night of beer, dope and more beer. As he tarries up the road toward me I realise that tonight will be the first time that anyone who knows Dec will meet someone who only knows Declan. Only Maet really knows me as both and, while I've told him all about Smithy, Smithy knows virtually nothing about any of the people that fill my week days.

Among the city workers darting to get home Smithy moves slower than most, all the while exhibiting more confidence in his relaxed swagger than middle managers on 150K do as they scurry toward the safety of a parking lot and their North Shore-bound European cars.

It takes less time to explain the ruse to Smithy than it took to convince Maet and in Smithy's can-do-anything presence the plan comes alive. If only his power was used for good and all that. I've told Maet that we'd meet him and Naomi B at the launch downtown.

'Pre-launch spliff?' Smithy asks needlessly as we take back streets to the bookshop that is hosting the launch of *Beauty Naturally* by US style guru and general powerhouse, Rhonda Kingi. I tell Smithy how Rhonda's agent warned Naomi B that the author eats like a bird, 'So Naomi B goes, "I'll make sure her portions are small" and the agent goes, "No I mean like a bird – nuts, seeds and sips of water".'

'I thought you were assigned the wacky books – what are they called?' Smithy surprises me that he remembers what I told him about MBS titles.

'Mind, Body, Spirit – apparently I'll take them over from Naomi B next season. At the moment I'm working on a chicks' type thing called *Mango Days*.'

'Damn fine,' Smithy says, practising an American accent.

We are met at the bookstore entrance by Naomi B, whose surreal blue eyes immediately decide not to waste any time scanning my face when they can feast on my companion. I go to introduce them but falter, unsure whether my mate is still Smithy or is already Jonson Weaver, and decide that as Smithy has not yet been briefed on his background it's safer that Naomi B and any other K&D people here meet Smithy tonight. Somehow I'll make sure they don't come along to see Weaver tomorrow night.

Leaving a stunned-by-Smithy Naomi B to greet guests we make our way over to Maet, who is deep in conversation by the drinks table. With Anna.

Maet steps into the breach, introducing himself and Anna to Smithy who, in support of me, under-whelms Anna with an indifferent nod. After explaining to Smithy, but for my info, that Anna is the editor for the Australian edition of *Beauty Naturally*, Maet beckons a food tray to float our way and take up some of the silence. From the array of double bite-sized snacks Maet takes a beef ball, Smithy collects three mini quiches and Anna and I simultaneously lunge for matching discs of fish cake.

Small talk is wrestled out of each of us in turn by Maet who fires questions around the group in a desperate attempt to forge a flowing conversation. Things take a turn, which way I'm not sure, when Anna laughs after I respond to Maet that for the inter-national food day at work I'm planning to bring chicken nuggets. Smithy gives me a wink to tell me I owe him, and I'm left wondering exactly who is and is not joking.

Anna, still chortling, says, 'I guess some people at work expect that I'll be bringing champagne and truffles.'

I rush to support her like Prince Valiant. 'Well, how lame are they if they judge you as a certain type simply because you live in a huge house and like expensive things?'

'No, I meant because I was born in France,' Anna explains.

I am so lame.

Anna rescues me. 'But I know what you mean Declan. There is nothing tastier than a chicken nugget and that holds true wherever you come from.'

Did I mention that I love her?

'I thought you just became a vegie?' Maet trivialises Anna's vision of a world united in its love of bite-sized bits of reconstituted chicken.

'I decided I'd give up meat for a year or so – it's sort of cool to throw yourself into another world now and then.'

Could it be that we are not such strangers after all?

Attention needs diverting so I ask Maet how his weekend of downsizing went. Maet becomes animated as he recounts how he discarded possessions in increasing volume and depth as the weekend progressed. I feel proud that he took my advice so seriously but concerned that his addiction to things might simply be replaced by an addiction to shedding them. The dilated pupils and feverish description of the buzz he gets from offloading possessions he once thought he cherished remind me of the euphoria a smack addict gets from each fix. After a crap day like today I won't be surprised if Maet goes home for the mother of all trips and tries to throw his house into the street.

Further insights into Maet's endeavours are interrupted when Naomi B carts over the author for a meet and greet. Ms Kingi then clamours aboard a makeshift rostrum to commence her short talk, which will be followed by questions from any of the forty-odd people surrounding the drinks table who remember why they're here.

Rhonda Kingi is totally ordinary in every way except for her nipples which, in the chill of the air-conditioning and held beneath nothing other than a tight white singlet, prove to be extraordinarily close to each other. She talks softly and deliberately, explaining her theories of inner beauty in the unnerving hushed tones of a funeral consultant. Before taking questions Naomi B asks Rhonda if she'd like a drink. Rhonda responds crisply. 'Water, no ice, thank you so much for asking.'

Question time runs smoothly and Smithy appears to be focused on the job at hand when he's not at the drinks table, food trays or Naomi B, who is so beguiled that she has even switched off her phone.

As soon as the official part of the night is over I whisk Smithy off. I don't need him conquering and discarding any of my work colleagues just yet and, more importantly, we need to make a start on turning him into Jonson Weaver for tomorrow night's launch, which is meant to be way more serious than tonight's little soiree.

Minutes out the door and I receive my second-ever call on my mobile.

'Just checking all is A-okay,' Maet seems to think that we are planning the world's largest bank heist and not one of Smithy's lesser scams.

'No worries – I'm taking Smithy home to brief him on his bio.'

'Yes Declan, she's still here.'

'What?' I respond confused.

'Yeah buddy, she is really nice.'

'What are you doing – is Anna with you?' I ask mortified.

'Uh-huh.'

'Shut the fuck up, Maet!'

'Have a nice night, dude,' Maet says cheerily and then he's gone.

'There are two reasons why these programmes do so well: 1 – We Americans have an insatiable appetite for the minutiae of life; and B – The escapism value of watching folk we judge to be our cultural inferiors cannot be underrated.'

Textbook response, except for the 1 and B bit, to my question.

Apart from a few glitches Smithy is cruising. He's playing with the audience's questions like a cat with so many mice. Charmed mice with no escape. Dressed in a hastily hired suit, speaking in generic American and having expounded for nearly twenty minutes on great moments from *Jerry Springer*, Smithy now settles into responding to his mesmerised fans' questions. Luckily after last night's bore fest Maet and I are the only ones from K&D in attendance. If by some fluke my job lasts much longer I won't need to hide Smithy away for the duration. The only print journo that was meant to be coming, Ashley from the *Daily Telegraph*, was cancelled by Maet – having a photograph of Smithy in the paper under the name of Jonson Weaver might be pushing our luck a bit far. 'Even if we could have swung it,' Maet told me in a whisper, 'I've got a more important story for Ash.'

Maet reckons every event has one. The feistiest member of this group of about seventy modern-culture vultures looks challengingly at Smithy and asks, 'How come you said before that it took you nearly two years to write the 100,000 words needed to complete this book but I've got a copy here and it only comes to 200 pages?'

'I used mostly short words.'

Good one Smithy, I think to myself.

While the audience laughs in support of the urbane Jonson Weaver, up jumps Maet who sensibly calls the Q and A to an abrupt end. All in all, though, I'm guessing Maet's been impressed by the way Smithy has weaved his talk to include the words closure, faucet, ketchup and diaper and mispronunciations of aluminium, semi-final, tomato and oregano.

A remarkably long queue starts to form at the signing table as Maet shuffles Jonson Weaver Smithy to meet his fans one by one. I wonder how these two will survive the next couple of days doing radio interviews without me along and I'm not comforted when mid-way through the snake of people Smithy jokingly complains of a sore hand and Maet snaps, 'Use your other one.'

25.

'How did Smithy take the news that you're going to move out?' Maet asks as soon as he opens his front door.

'Incredibly calmly, but he was pretty stoned. I told him on the way home from fish and chips at his parents' place. It was that combo of disappointed but not surprised, like waking up with someone you'd picked up the previous night and all you can see is bed hair. He even offered to help me look today but I told him that you'd offered to guide me round.'

'He comes across as so hard to please but I reckon he's a lot easier-going than he makes out. Taking him around the radio stations last week was a breeze – but I'm guessing he doesn't know I'm gay.' Maet says. 'Does he?'

'Nope,' I respond, embarrassed to admit to Maet that I've hidden the fact from my best friend. That it is even an issue.

I check out Maet's house for the first time as he leads me through toward the small back courtyard.

Everything seems compact but it's not nearly as neat as Jerry Seinfeld's place. Lucky Maet's been caught up in a frenzy of minimalism, as I can't imagine how you'd squeeze in much furniture.

'Where does the inner west begin?' I ask as we stop in the stainless steel mini-kitchen to grab some juice. Here the appliances are infinitely smaller than their older relatives living large and white in Sydney's outer suburbs.

'Anywhere the aeroplanes cast a shadow longer than your backyard.'

Given that I can see Maet's patch of green is too small to sustain a dieting guinea pig I assume this house is pretty well inner west central.

Inside Maet's mini-fridge the impact of his new 'less is more' philosophy is evident. He's definitely a ten items or less express-lane case. Hand basket only. The few items that have managed to survive the selection process proudly declare themselves to be either single-serve or 'fun-size'. I'm here in Tokyo or Lilliput.

Spreading the newspaper over his intimate outdoor setting and opening at the 'Share Accommodation' pages, Maet grabs his only pen (having explained how long a single pen can last) and circles the suburbs we'll target, ones close to work so I can walk.

'How about this one – why'd you skip these?' I say pointing to one advertisement.

Maet laughs. 'Very funny – "Broadminded" is not an actual place.'

'Okay, where's your phone?' I ask.

'We'll have to use a mobile – I got rid of the landline.'

'Fuck, you've really taken to this big time, haven't you?'

'No mucking around. I've even found a website devoted to minimalism and made friends with a girl I met there. We email each other with reports of what we've gotten rid of – it's becoming pretty competitive. Last I heard she'd reduced her name from Annalise to Anna, then Ana and now she signs off as merely A. She reckons she's never felt so liberated.'

'You're obsessed.' I tease.

'Speaking of which, did you notice that yesterday both you and your Anna removed the tofu from your laksa?' Maet has a bit of Sherlock in him as well.

'The question is, did my Anna notice?' I say, thinking perhaps I'll make shared-tofu-removal my Anna highlight for the past week.

'Don't know. Meanwhile it's time to start calling some of these numbers. Here's one that sounds right: "Alexandria – shared house seeks meat-eating smoker who hates pets",' Maet says with a smile.

I grab his phone and dial the number. The answering machine takes my call.

'Hello. I am Oliver's answering machine. What are you?'

I hang up.

'Wanker.'

'No worries, here's another: "Glebe – fun house with three others, furnished room, available immediately".'

A girl answers.

'Hi, my name's Dec, I'm calling about the room – can I come and have a look?'

'Well Dex, we're here all day so rock over whenever. The address is 18 Brighton Street.'

'Dec,' I note, writing down the address.

'Dex is it?'

'Sure. Okay.'

'Great, see you later today then,' she says vaguely and hangs up.

'I'll wait in the car,' Maet announces as we pull up as close to the house as possible.

'Why?'

'They might think I'm your boyfriend,' he says with a wink.

'I don't care.' I'll decide later if that's really true.

'Well, they might have a problem with it. It's no biggie. Good luck.' Maet reclines his driver's seat for a snooze in the air-conditioned comfort as I start the walk past rows of small attached terraces, baking in the midday sun, to number eighteen.

The most noticeable feature from the street is

that a huge fridge is sat on the porch, only metres from the pavement, presumably because it doesn't fit through the front door. For a second I guess that it has been dumped until a break between planes allows me to make out the familiar hum of cooling food. As I knock on the door I step on the power cord that runs into a mouse hole cut out of the door's base.

'Hey, Dex isn't it?' says the girl who opens the door. She doesn't sound vague now.

'Yeah, how'd you know?' I respond impressed.

'Yours was the only inquiry we got,' she replies matter-of-factly but with no hint of disappointment. 'My name's Eliza. Come through and I'll introduce you to the others.'

Eliza has fair skin and blonde-to-white hair but her Nordic look is broken by chocolate-coloured eyes surrounded by dark lashes. As we walk via the living and dining rooms to the kitchen, I feel comforted by the disarray.

'I don't know what I've cooked,' says a serious-looking girl with hair like Andre Agassi used to have. She's staring at a tray of clumps fresh from the oven as we enter the kitchen.

Eliza introduces me to the surprised chef. 'Heidi this is Dex, Dex Heidi.'

'Hi,' I say as Heidi tosses the lot into the bin.

'Heidi is a biscuit designer,' Eliza offers as way of explanation.

I smile.

Heidi doesn't.

After Heidi leaves the kitchen, furious at her failure, Eliza whispers to me: 'A very unhappy lesbian.'

As Eliza turns to show me upstairs, where somehow they've squeezed in three bedrooms, a guy slips into the kitchen without saying a word and deposits a half-consumed cup of coffee in the microwave, then repeatedly tries to enter what appears to be a four-digit password.

'Travis, you're at home, that's the microwave, press reheat – one minute,' Eliza says.

'Cheers,' Travis replies listlessly. He is tall and lanky like an IT professional.

'Travis is an IT professional,' Eliza informs me. 'Travis, this is Dex.'

'Cheers,' Travis says and shakes my hand loosely.

Every person at some point stops keeping up with fashion trends. For Travis it was 1992. Watching his black stonewash jeans and white high-top sneakers ascend the stairs I wonder, where does he find replacements?

Eliza shows me my room, which overlooks the small back garden that leads to a narrow laneway. The room already has a bed and a rack to hang clothes so if I get the place I can leave my bed for Rat-Boy, who can't wait to take my room at Smithy's.

'So, do you want to move in?' Eliza asks.

'Just like that – don't you want to discuss it with the others?' I'm nervous at how fast this is moving.

Eliza responds kindly. 'If you're happy with us we're happy with you.' Perhaps she's desperate.

'Sure,' I say, though I'm not entirely. 'One-twenty-five a week and share food and bills, isn't it?'

'Yep, you can move in today if you like.'

'Maybe tomorrow if that's alright – my mate Smithy's going to help me, though I really don't have much stuff.'

'Well, that's good. As you've probably noticed, there's not much room anyways.'

Deal done we leave my room. Eliza points out Travis' door next to mine and at the front end of the house the only other upstairs door. 'That's mine and Heidi's room.'

I went to bed in my room and wake up in Rat-Boy's bed. My last night as a Bankstown resident was spent much the same way as the previous five thousand. Between Smithy's pre-final-night-at-home spliffs and pre-moving-out spliffs we each drank our way through at least a dozen VBs. Smithy certainly put a brave face on it and maybe the fact that I didn't, beer over-flow welling in my blurred eyes, ensured that Smithy retains his place as our leader, steady and sure.

Maya's baby, one month till launch date, kicked at

her ruthlessly between gulps of Coke while Rat-Boy, celebrating his good fortune to be soon leaving Mustafa and Zahra, passed out early and was collected by his older brother, who now finally has a room to himself.

Conversation trickles as Smithy drives me to Glebe in a car I think even he doesn't know who owns.

'Convenient,' he comments as he double-parks directly outside my new home and acknowledges the placement of the white goods. 'What stops people just helping themselves to the food?'

'I've no idea,' I answer honestly.

I introduce Smithy to Eliza who explains the others are both out for the afternoon. For once a female doesn't tremble at the knees for him but he seems not to notice. We unload the pile of clothes that I didn't even bother to box and a laundry bag that holds the rest of my material life and for a minute I want to fuck the job, fuck this place, fuck it all. But I'll play on for the car. I want it all.

Neither Smithy nor I make a fuss when he leaves. For my part I'm hoping that nothing between us need change. He's never asked me why I had to get a job or leave our home – which is good, because I've no idea.

'So is that your boyfriend?' Eliza asks as I start to sort my room.

I laugh and turn to see if Smithy is laughing too but I'm not at home.

'No, I'm straight,' I say, hoping my laughter is not construed as a put down.

To take my mind off the fact that it is six in the evening and my friends will be at the pub I decide to explore my new world, walking towards the city, taking the path that fate decrees, crossing the road if the light is green or if there is a break in the traffic. My new local corner store is decorated in the same dust that is used so heavily by Bankstown shop-keepers and features a window display based solely on a few bottles of Coke and a sign advertising bread rolls – twenty cents each or five for a dollar. A couple of kids are kicking a frozen chicken along the road till it falls apart. I guess it could have come from our fridge. The sun's glare is fading enough to allow a tribe of goths to venture out in their heavy black coverings that see them taking to summer like cats to water. All the while, every few blocks, I notice a real cat, different each time, like living pieces of street furniture. Acting as sentries. They pretend not to clock you, or at the least look as though they don't care, but each couple of blocks there's another one. I've no idea how they communicate with each other.

26.

This week I've only had three meals – if you count a meal as a combination of at least two ingredients. Noodles alone is not a meal, a kebab is. And although it's only Wednesday in my first week of life outside of Bankstown I've already replaced one set of rituals with another. Instead of dope, my mates and the pub, I now spend the day looking forward to chocolate, Nirvana and a wank. They say the good thing about masturbation is that you don't have to look your best, but I'm keen for the time when my sex life might again include a second person – preferably Anna – and I can reinstall handbrake images of Margaret Thatcher or Lisa Curry Kenny.

My new number one haircut allows me to continue shampoo rationing without my hair appearing too greasy – which I classify as more positive than simply giving up on Anna by washing my hair normally. The water that slides through this old house's pipes, down our bodies and occasionally over the dishes is so rusty that I think the iron content might make my hair grow back at twice the speed. Maybe short hair, a new look, will be the clincher with Anna. I've nothing to lose, as it's half way through the week already and no candidate for most-significant-Anna-moment has revealed itself.

It's barely nine pm and, as I lay on my bed staring at the blades of the ceiling fan, watching how they slow down when you pick a particular one and follow it round, I know that my next conscious moment will be coming to just as Triple J's morning weather report has skipped past Sydney's forecast.

Preparing for another day at work based on the fact that it will be 27 degrees in Perth, I decide to go with white T-shirt and jeans. My first stint of sequential days of non-alcohol-induced sleep is playing havoc with my usual routine of not having the time or inclination even to consider what to wear. I check my toothbrush, and discover it's wet again even though I've not used it for 24 hours and the toothpaste, like the soap, never seems to diminish. It's as if Smithy has set the residents of this place a toiletries-restriction challenge. Who the fuck is using my toothbrush?

Travis has already been to the mini-mart but the plastic carrier bag of food sits discarded on the kitchen floor with what appears to be milk and egg combining to form a puddle beneath it.

'Sorry about the mess, Dex. I was swinging the bag as I waited on the kerb to cross and a car smashed into my shopping mid-swing. Fucking narrow streets.'

In way of support I pour Travis a juice into one of Heidi's crystal goblets, given to her an age ago by some old relative for her glory box, and now given a lease of life whenever all the other glasses have been used.

'Still on for tonight?' Maet says as I slump into my seat.

'Tonight?' I ask, still dazed from my walk to work in what already must be 34 degrees.

'Dinner at your place. Me, Naomis A and B, and possibly another friend of mine. I asked Maxine but it seems she and this Sebastian guy are on some sort of fitness kick and go for a run each night. Dec, we organised this on Monday to get you started in your new home. Remember?'

As I recall Maet did mention something along these lines, but I think saying that we 'organised' it is a bit much. For Maet and his friends dinner parties are as regular as Western tourists in India but for me and my mates eating, drinking and talking simultaneously is pretty well unheard of, unless it's in the presence of a television or a bong. I don't think Maet truly comprehends how unentertaining my friends and I are.

'Sure, no worries,' I say, the smallest gust of enthusiasm starting to brew. At least I'll be distracted from thinking about what my mates are doing for one night. I even contemplate asking Smithy, Maya and Rat-Boy along, but decide it's too soon to merge old and new – though I could do with one or three of Smithy's pre-dinner party spliffs. Anyway, we only have five chairs and probably bugger-all food.

'Declan, it's a Sid Farkis on line three for you.' Naomi on Reception is chirping through the phone.

'Hey, Smithy,' I say.

'Thought I'd catch a train in to town for a look around,' Smithy lies. 'Want to meet up at that pub near your offices for a few bevies?'

'Fuck yeah.'

'See ya at four.'

I check with Maet that it's okay to leave early and he assumes it's to prepare for dinner. I say nothing as I don't wish to disappoint – there's time enough for that later when he sits down to eat.

Smithy has a spliff at the ready when I collect him from the bus shelter outside Universal Tower. We take a detour down a side street to smoke the joint before surfacing at the pub, nicely primed for a few beers. For the first time that I can remember we find ourselves filling each other in on news that is more than 24 hours old. It's four days since we last spoke, and it sure feels like we have a lot to catch up on.

'What ya been up to?' I ask.

'Not much – did some work on Sascha's flat the other day.'

'Did she pay you?'

'Nah, but she said I can use the computer that what's-his-face left behind when he dumped her.'

'What do you want with a computer?' I ask. Even at work I avoid the machine as much as I can.

'Dunno – I've been getting into the internet. Checking out the sites. You can waste fucking days, dude,' declares one waster of decades to another.

'Maya alright?'

'Yep, just over three weeks to go.'

'How's Rat-Boy?'

'Happy as a fucking lark,' Smithy says between swigs of VB.

For weeks Smithy has seemed indifferent to my new life, even at times mildly supportive, so I am almost relieved when, finally he takes a jab. 'Yep, Rat-Boy is not about to ditch his mates.'

'Is that what you think about me?'

'Just joshing, we still see too much of ya.' Smithy saves face and gives me a friendly punch on the shoulder.

My first beers in the best part of a week seem to be going to my head and I almost cheer when Smithy casually suggests that I should come back to Banks-town for the weekend to stay on Jeff's sofa.

Why did I think he'd make it hard for me to keep what I had? Cause I'm a fucking idiot that's why.

'Full Dec?' Smithy says, grinning at my blurry eyes.

'Uh-huh. Fuck, what's the time?' I shriek.

Smithy checks my mobile. 'Six-thirty.'

'Work people are coming over for dinner at my place in half an hour. Shit!'

'Are *you* cooking?' Smithy asks, incredulous.

'I was going to get takeaway and chuck it into Heidi's glory-box serving dishes but I've only got enough money for a taxi now. It's just Maet and a couple of Naomis so I don't really need to impress. I'm going to have to wing it with what's in the fridge – there was a frozen chook but last I saw it was flying through a set of goal posts.'

Smithy must reckon I'm even more pissed than I look.

'See ya tomorrow night,' I say and leave him in the pub.

My taxi pulls up outside my house just in time for me to catch a glimpse of Eliza letting in my workmates: Maet, Naomi A, Naomi B . . . and Anna!

Momentarily it crosses my mind to ask the driver to continue on to Bankstown but I decide to have a quick look in the fridge before I join my guests inside. The freezer is mostly frozen over and only has room for a tub of Neapolitan ice-cream and a massive bag of chicken drumsticks. The fridge houses yet more chicken drumsticks and a range of old condiments, wilting vegetables and brightly coloured beverages. Eliza, ears peeled for the sound of fridge raiders, joins me on the front porch as I shake my head at the poor excuse for a larder.

'Do you know that you have four people inside who claim you're preparing dinner for them?'

I explain my predicament and Eliza goes into crisis-management mode.

'Grab the bottle of Coke and the chicken drumsticks – the unfrozen ones – and take them through to the kitchen. Your guests brought some bottles of white wine. If I turn off the air-conditioner, they'll drink quickly and get so pissed they won't know how hungry they are.'

I slink past the front room with the ingredients for who-knows-what, ignoring Maet's cries of hello. After dumping the stuff in the kitchen I join everyone as Eliza is merrily uncorking two bottles of wine at once. Anna stands up graciously and shakes my hand. 'Hi Declan, I hope you don't mind me coming. Maet said you had cooked heaps and needed extras.'

'That's cool,' I say. I'm melting and not just because the air-conditioning is off.

Maet is grinning at me and in my still-intoxicated state I leer back at him just a little too comically.

'Well, I'd better get back to the kitchen,' I slur. 'Eliza, can you join me for a sec?'

'Oh Declan, sorry but I don't drink alcohol – anything cold would be great,' Anna says softly as I'm halfway out the doorway.

'No worries,' I say worried.

Again Eliza and I meet at the fridge, by the street, in the shit.

Eliza confirms the worst as she stares into the battered fridge. 'I need all the Coke for the meal, she doesn't drink wine, and you can't give her brown water. She has a choice: "Mountain Blast" Powerade or mixed-berry drinking yoghurt.'

'This is a girl who has probably eaten in the finest restaurants and been to hundreds of elegant dinner parties and tonight madam can select her beverage of choice as long as it is either a luminescent blue sports drink or a lilac-coloured milky digestive?' I'm crumbling.

'She did say anything cold would be great. Do you fancy her?'

'Yes.' Isn't it fucking obvious?

Anna chooses the yoghurt drink, which I pour into the last remaining crystal goblet before joining Eliza in the kitchen as she fills our largest saucepan with two litres of Coke and as many drumsticks as can be submerged in it.

'You just boil away till the Coke evaporates and

the drumsticks are cooked,' she explains matter-of-factly.

I'm in no position to argue so await further instructions.

'Given that the table is going to look bare I think we should put out dessert at the same time. People will hop in before it melts in this heat. Go and grab the ice-cream from the fridge.'

I look in on my guests to make sure all is okay. The Naomis are really throwing back the wine. Soon enough, I hope, they'll be entertaining the lot of us.

Eliza peels the lid off the Neapolitan tub to reveal the worst – the entire chocolate and strawberry columns have been skillfully removed leaving just vanilla, languishing in inferiority.

'Not a problem,' she says, 'Scoop it all into one of Heidi's special serving dishes and stuff some of these macadamia nuts into it. They'll think it's gourmet ice-cream.'

'I hope no one's a fucking closet diabetic,' I say. Then again, a seizure might divert attention from the scarcity of real food. And where did she find the nuts?

By the time the chicken has triumphed over the Coke the Naomis are singing Eminem tracks verbatim, Anna is onto her third goblet of drinking yoghurt and Maet is rabbiting on about the success of the Jonson Weaver tour. Eliza decides not to join us for dinner, but I decide not to worry. Most likely she's realised there aren't enough chairs and definitely not enough food for six.

My workmates, inexplicably, have seated themselves in the dining room as if they are in some television sit-com – all squeezed around one side of the oval table so the camera crew can film them. Then I realize that someone has activated the air-conditioning and my well-cooked guests have huddled as close to the chilled breeze as possible.

The very moment I present the drumsticks coincides with the instant my brain recalls the fact that Anna has just commenced her year-long tryst with vegetarianism. But she cuts me off as I start to apologise, 'Thank goodness – I am *so* sick of fish and vegetables!'

The Naomis barely eat a thing and no one seems to notice how light on the food is – nice as they taste, there are two drumsticks left over. Mostly the chat is about work and Anna loses no points by remaining diplomatic as the Naomis slag off everybody who is not at the table. After her second helping of gourmet ice-cream Anna says that she must be going, thanking me for a fun night. Suddenly Naomi B wakes with a start and, through her cascading dark ringlets, declares, 'You're better off without him Anna, that's what I say.'

As Naomi B slumps back against Naomi A the

look on my face causes Anna to tell me and Maet that her boyfriend, the angry wheelchair guy, broke it off with her last night. Fucking idiot.

'I'm actually surprised how much of a relief it is,' she says, reading my mind.

Thursday night and we have the certain winner of most significant Anna moment of the week.

27.

The more I think about Maya's baby the less I think about Jeff. As the baby grows Jeff diminishes. Soon the baby will join us. Will Jeff disappear completely then? What do Smithy and I do when we have nothing of Jeff, not even jarring reminders? Who am I if not someone who lost his mate and struggles to move along?

When I invited Smithy over to Maet's place tonight for drinks followed by a trip to the local pub for a trivia night he surprised me by being all for it. Maybe his stint as an author wasn't just for my benefit after all. Have I been too fucking self-absorbed to realise I'm not the only one who wants to try different things, different people?

Even though Maet has asked about ten people from work it is really just a smokescreen for his continuing endeavour to help me get to know Anna. I'm impressed by his persistence – I wouldn't want to go up against him in a toiletries-restriction competition. He'd stink.

As I wait to meet Smithy on Erskineville Station the wind blows so frantically that even my short hair seems to ruffle. I imagine Maxine's would lash out at low-flying birds. Then again it might just stay perfectly intact, in cool defiance of the conditions around it.

'Pre-quiz spliff?' Smithy asks as he ambles off the train.

'Thanks, dude.'

I fill in Smithy on the people he'll meet at Maet's, besides our host, Anna and Naomi B who he's already met: two more Naomis, Maxine, Goat and Emma from Marketing, Kurt Cobain from Sales and a couple of Anna's colleagues from Editorial who are generally known as the 'new young guys from Editorial'.

We are the last to arrive at Maet's place and it appears he'd have run out of chairs even if only people named Naomi were invited. Kurt is wrapping up a short speech congratulating Maet on the sales of Jonson Weaver's book since his successful tour. Smithy winks at Maet, who somehow avoids cracking up.

'How's the excess clutter problem going?' I ask Maet unnecessarily when the back-slapping is over.

'Brilliant, thanks to you and A. Got rid of my bed yesterday, just a trumped-up mattress holder. I'm still buzzing from that one.' His eyes are glowing.

The Goat rudely checks, within the entire group's earshot, with those he's invited to his annual supper that they are still coming, bypassing Naomi on Reception and the new young guys from Editorial. Surprisingly all invitees are eager although Maxine has to pass on Sebastian's behalf as he'll be tied up that night. I've said yes on Maet's advice that, while it's a drag to schlep to Neutral Bay and Goat is a complete wanker, the food and wine are supposed to be excellent. And when I realise Anna is going, I don't care if Goat only serves cucumber sandwiches.

With Goat keeping a firm grip of the talking stick we are all led into a conversation about the joys of European travel. I can tell that Anna could find her way from Milan to Minsk but she lets Goat do all the bleating. Seeing the faces of the group glaze, Smithy decides to wonder aloud why tourists, especially old ones, video themselves staggering through fifteen countries in as many days.

'Who are these films for – some of these guys are down to their last toothbrush and still they are trying to immortalise themselves. Surely it's up to those they leave behind to design the memory. If you really prized someone you'd create your own tribute.'

I get it, I think Maet does, I hope Anna does, Maxine just might, the rest drift from glazed to blank.

After Smithy's group-discussion death-blow the gang disseminates as sparsely as Maet's narrow living room allows. Anna gets trapped by Goat across the room, I find myself sat on the only sofa with Maxine, while nearby Naomi on Reception forms a huddle with Smithy. Maxine doesn't seem to mind that I maintain a superficial dialogue with her so I can simultaneously listen in on Smithy and Naomi on Reception, ensuring my mate doesn't launch any more radical theories. Indeed Maxine appears happy to have a bit of an eavesdrop herself. It's a skill, having a chat while listening in on another. Some chicks are famous for it.

For some reason Naomi on Reception has decided Smithy needs to know that in her opinion most people at K&D, especially Guy Murdoch, aka Goat, think that she is thick and useless simply because she answers the telephone and does the mail. As tears glisten in her eyes, Smithy, so rarely chosen to be a shoulder to cry on, makes use of the same cornered expression I selected to wear for the duration of my dinner party last week. To enhance his discomfort Naomi on Reception announces that the new young bloke in Editorial, the Asian-looking one, has replaced the eleven o'clock courier in her affections.

Kindly, Smithy doesn't cut and run but instead does his best to steer the conversation to topics he's more comfortable with, namely science and nature. As Maxine and I give up any pretence of not listening in, Smithy regales Naomi on Reception with semi-interesting facts about how smart Japanese crows are, or the more bizarre causes of death in the South Pacific.

Naomi on Reception looks desperate when Maet finally starts herding us out the door for the walk down his street to The Erskineville. It seems she thought we were just having drinks and the idea of being part of a trivia team is freaking her out. Naomis A and B escort her along the pavement assuring her that they're no smarter than she is.

We score the last free table, at the very front of the main bar. Manoeuvring myself between Anna and Goat I hope to win a few points from a relieved Anna but she is oblivious. There are ten tables in all and the initial debates at each are about what to call the team. Goat's imaginative suggestion – 'K&D' – is seconded by lack of interest and passed unanimously.

Smithy is held up with the drinks as the bar manager fusses with the telephone and several baying customers. The Naomis have already grabbed a bunch of Vodka Cruisers the minute they walked in the door – good thing too, as Naomi on Reception now looks less of a flight risk.

'Seems the trivia host hasn't fronted,' Smithy reports when he finally returns with our VBs.

'So is the quiz cancelled?' I ask.

Smithy says, flashing a grin. 'Nope. I volunteered, so you're going to have to make do without me.'

'What do you have to do?' How can Smithy be so adventurous when he rarely leaves an area smaller than most battleships?

'There's a book of questions. I just have to keep a record of which ones I've asked and jot down the answers for the bar staff who do the scoring. See ya.'

Smithy grabs his beer, the book and a microphone, and brings the house to order.

The first set of twenty questions, in the race for the grand prize of a hundred Erko dollars, redeemable for food and beverages at this pub only, go well for most tables but not K&D. Goat, our self-appointed team captain, is feeling a little let-down by his team members and his chief target for frowns is Naomi on Reception, who to date has not offered a single suggested answer for consideration, even for questions about celebrities or fashion.

At the start of the second and final round Smithy confirms the scores – we languish in third-last position.

'Round two, question one. What is the fifth-leading cause of death in Fiji?'

Maxine looks over at me, her face wrinkling slightly. A smile.

'I know this!' Naomi on Reception almost screams. 'I heard or read about it just recently. It's being hit on the head by a coconut!'

Goat looks around the group for alternatives and then back to Naomi on Reception. 'Are you sure? Sounds far-fetched to me.'

'I'm sure.' Naomi on Reception says, and then hesitates. 'I think.'

'We'll put it down for now,' says Goat. 'We can

change it later if anyone comes up with something else.'

Smithy returns to the script and K&D continues to stumble along but I notice Naomi on Reception starts to offer answers for every other question. A legitimate-sounding question about Johnny Depp has both me and Anna responding 'What's Eating Gilbert Grape?' in unison. Most significant Anna moment for this week secured.

'And finally, question twenty.' Smithy takes a deep breath. 'How do Japanese Carrion crows crack the shells of nuts so they can eat them?'

This one rings a bell as well.

Goat looks stupefied as Naomi on Reception whispers, 'They put them under the wheels of cars at traffic lights and collect them after the cars have run over them. They are very intelligent birds,' she adds for effect.

'Not the only ones,' Maxine says, nodding toward Goat then the new Asian-looking young guy from Editorial.

After the answer cards have been collected and marked by the bar staff Smithy reads out the correct answers and the final scores. Unsurprisingly Naomi on Reception scores a couple of big hits, getting thumbs up from Goat both times. K&D limps in fourth but as Smithy declares to his second live audience in as many weeks, 'We're all winners on the night.'

28.

After Smithy's triumph as quizmaster the other night, Goat asked me to invite him along to his annual supper. It's sort of ironic that I get to bring a male friend and Maet doesn't.

Smithy's first reaction was blunt – 'I'm not going over the fucking bridge' – but after I explained about the catering he relented pretty damn quickly. Maet offered to collect him from Erskineville Station then come get me before we headed for enemy territory.

I get in Maet's car just as he and Smithy are discussing Maxine. Maet is telling Smithy about that popular email she doctored and sent to selected staff, entitling it 'How to Spot Guy Murdoch' and including an unflattering photo of Goat alongside the quote: *If you see two people talking and one looks bored, he's the other one.*

Even though, to my knowledge, he's never seen an email Smithy laughs and asks me what I think of the lady who gave me my first-ever job.

'She's always been nice enough to me, but I think

she might be pretty lonely outside of work. A few times I've noticed her abscond with food left over from meetings, and next morning the empty trays are in her office. Maybe it's just her appetite since she gave up smoking. I'm glad she's got this Sebastian dude in her life now.'

'Sebastian's a Maltese terrier,' Smithy states matter-of-factly. 'Buddy, I thought you were meant to be more Sherlock than that.'

'A dog!' Maet and I blurt simultaneously.

'How do you know?' I ask.

'We got to talking after the trivia night – she admitted that she purposely keeps details about Sebastian hazy because she likes people thinking she has a man in her life,' Smithy says, enlightening a couple of thickheads who only happen to see this lady every friggin' week day.

Suddenly Smithy is surfing the net, signing books, hosting quizzes and having heart-to-hearts with female executives. I thought I was the one who'd moved on.

'And when will you two be seeing each other again?' I ask sarcastically.

'Apart from tonight you mean?'

'Yeah.' Maybe he likes her.

'Well, she suggested that the four of us go on a double-date thing.'

'The four of us?' I glance nervously at Maet.

'Me and her, you and Anna, stupid.'

'What!' I screech in time with Maet's tyres as he again forgets to focus on his driving.

'Dude, it's time to wash your hair.'

'Welcome to the North Side,' Goat says, yellowed eyes twinkling in the glare of the powerful street lighting that he and fellow-residents of this patch of Neutral Bay no doubt campaigned for. The three of us enter the gargantuan house, stepping into a gleaming foyer dripping with elegance and, to Maet's horror, truck-loads of other more tangible stuff. I'm guessing there's family money on show here. K&D remuneration is not that good.

'Let me introduce Perfect,' Goat says, and motions over a small, fragile woman who I assume to be his wife.

While we joked her name might be Nanny, I certainly didn't expect it to be Perfect – overkill, surely, even for the upper-middle classes.

'Did you say Perfect?' Silent thanks to Smithy for asking that on behalf of all of us.

Mrs Goat's answer is belligerent but composed. 'Sorry, that's Guy's little joke. A lifetime ago when we finished high school our yearbook misprinted the word 'prefect' under my photo. Guy's hung on to that one for more than twenty years.'

We still don't catch her real name. She seems to

be suffering from the flu. Her nose is all red and has been threatening to release a fat drop on the sparkling white tiles since we arrived.

'It can't have been that long ago, babe,' Goat implores.

Mrs Goat faces us and under a cupped hand whispers loudly: 'Guy is having difficulty dealing with being forty. I've told him that Tom Cruise is over forty but he assures me that would only help if I were a little more Penelope Cruz.'

After spluttering into a concealed handkerchief, Mrs Goat fidgets with stray strands from an otherwise perfect French roll as her husband announces her, to a freshly arrived Kurt, as his wife. This woman's real name is a greater mystery than Jack the Ripper's.

Finally we are shown through to a room referred to as 'The Library' where four walls of oak shelves strain under the weight of at least a thousand dusty hardcovers most likely bought by the metre.

The collection of guests, which includes numerous people who don't work at K&D, have already started on the platters of mini-morsels that have been set on the wooden bureau at the centre of the National Library of Goat. Our host motions to his nameless wife that she should introduce us recent arrivals to our fellow grazers. On being introduced to a couple called The Pratts, Goat, from the other side of the room, hypocritically cries, 'What is this? *Bewitched*?

Their names are Miles and Fiona – maybe you should go and see to your nose, honey.'

As we shake hands with the embarrassed Pratts, Mrs Goat excuses herself, needlessly explaining she has a cold. I picture her having another good old swig at the flu medicine.

Maxine and Anna join us just as Goat herds us all into yet another room, but not before I see Maxine flash Smithy a smile she's been storing away for at least a month and a half. After skillfully securing a seat next to Anna I ask for directions to the bathroom so I can check nothing green has settled between my front teeth for the night. Choosing one of the four bathrooms offered by Goat I catch a glimpse of myself in the mirror and see a plastic fake smile plastered over my face. I splash cold water on the smile in an attempt to destroy it – which works, thank goodness, as the other option was to take a bite out of the guest soap. A quick survey of the near-spotless bathroom as I take a leak reveals two interesting clues to a better understanding of goat life. High up on the tiles above the cistern are two concentrations of smudged fingerprints. They are too high to be those of the little missus, so I deduce that our Marketing Manager regularly has trouble standing upright as he takes a piss. Second point of interest is the huge bag of Spanish onions that sits propped behind the door.

The purpose of the onions is still troubling me as I run into Mrs Goat in the hallway. I can see that she's been crying.

'What's the matter?' I ask.

'Nothing. Really. Just a little wound up.'

'If you think a smoke might help, Smithy and I will be partaking in your backyard after mains,' I say, taking the risk that she's not an undercover narc.

'That would be great – thanks,' she replies and leads me back to the dining room.

'Well, well. Declan and my sweetheart. Should I be worried?' Goat jokes as we take our seats at the largest dining table to be found outside a royal residence.

Neither of us bothers to respond and I raise my eyebrows at Anna, all the while messaging my smile to stay natural. She actually returns the gesture. Thing is, she seems no more comfortable about being drenched in formality than I am. As promised, the food is delicious and as hoped the company sublime. Anna and I get to chat loads even though it is still mostly work-based. She tells me that she's been given *Mango Days* to work on, deciding on an Australian jacket and jazzing up the look for the local market. When I tell her that this title will be my first tour Anna genuinely seems pleased that we'll be working together. I check her glass and recall that she does not drink alcohol so unless she's dropped an E before coming tonight there's a chance she might like me. And suddenly the possibility of me asking her out, and saving my hair, seems a distinct option.

After a spliff, that is.

My night-time daydreaming is interrupted by Goat raving on about the bastards who recently stole his new Bang and Olufsen CD/DVD stereo system with large screen plasma TV, before he had chance to insure it. This after his complaint that the house we are all currently being swamped by is too small for him and 'the trouble and strife' and all their things. Maet cringes as Goat lists the crap he plans to purchase, items that will require, for their comfort, a larger residence.

'Guy is one of those hunter and gatherer types.' Mrs Goat leans over to me and Anna. 'He hunts through catalogues and gathers at the mall.'

We both smile as Goat calls for more wine.

'I think you've whined enough, Guy,' says Mrs Goat.

Immediately after mains Goat suggests we change seats so we can mingle. Given the size of the table this is probably a sensible suggestion, but as I'm currently next to Anna it's a fucking crap idea. Maxine and Smithy also seem hesitant to heed Goat's call but booze has made him insistent. As luck would have it I score him and Fiona Pratt as my new slices of bread.

Inquisitiveness finally gets the better of me. I ask

Goat the purpose of the bag of onions in bathroom number three.

'My wife plants things that she·uses all the time throughout the house. It forces her to walk more than you normally would – it's in place of an exercise programme. There are onions in the bathroom, toothpaste in the kitchen, telephone books in the laundry, canned food in the back garden.' Goat looks exasperated.

To my right Fiona Pratt is talking with her husband across the table in forced, oh-so-polite tones. Perhaps it's just that I've seen the Goats in action, but I decide maybe a bit of argy-bargy is a better indicator of a healthy marriage than formal civility.

Smithy throws a pea at me to say it's time for a spliff.

'Just going for a smoke,' I say to Goat, implying cigarette but requiring dope, and give Mrs Goat the nod. Discreetly, she follows me and Smithy to the kitchen, where she unloads an empty salad bowl, then continues out the back with us. Smithy doesn't seem surprised that we have company and merrily lights up a massive joint. After a few tokes Mrs Goat loosens up and chooses to surprise us with the news that all is not great between her and her husband.

'I'm pretty sure he was actually going to end it the other day. He asked me to meet him for lunch – he never does that. When I arrived at the restaurant his car was out front and I noticed he'd only forked out for fifteen minutes parking. I left immediately and by the time he got home that night he was plastered and had probably forgotten the whole business.'

'And he hasn't mentioned it since?' I ask, dragging deeply on the spliff.

'No, and before you ask I'm not planning on staying around. But I refuse to have him dump me. I want to leave when it suits me.' She's quite feisty for one so petite.

Smithy, trying to change the subject, asks how much the nicked Bang and Olufsen stuff cost.

'Twelve grand, I think.' Mrs Goat sounds unconcerned.

'You guys could replace it for much less than that on ebay,' suggests Smithy, the new internet junkie. 'Get your husband to check out the site – I think I've seen systems like it for about five grand, no more than that.'

'Actually five grand is what I got for it.' Mrs Goat giggles.

'You stole it?' I whisper.

'Well it was ours, not just his. I didn't do it for the money. I was just sick of his obsession with buying the latest of everything – a life devoted to updating. So I put it up for auction on the net and it went for just over five grand. It was uninsured, so he was the only one to lose.'

'If you didn't want the money why didn't you just put it out on the street while he was at work? It wouldn't have lasted two minutes, not even around here.'

'I did, but a neighbour must have grabbed it for safekeeping and returned it to the front door just before Guy was due home.'

'That was right neighbourly,' Smithy says.

'Not really, more scared into submission. Guy made such a fuss in the neighbourhood a few months back when we left an antique table in the front yard for five minutes and it was snatched. The repairer had called on his mobile to say he was passing in his van, so we left it out for him. Guy was furious, going from door to door trying to discover who thought we were throwing it out because of a scratched leg. We never got it back but the neighbours were certainly warned.'

Smithy has a suggestion. 'If you still don't want the dirty money, we'll take it off your hands.'

'No we won't!' I insist.

'No dude, not for us. I was thinking about Maet's idea of getting one of those city park benches dedicated to Jeff. I read on the net that they cost nearly ten grand a piece.'

'Even if you pay the money,' I say, 'they still only go to society types not to regular people.'

Mrs Goat finishes off the joint and stubs the roach

on a tray of canned baked beans that has found its way into the backyard. She stands shakily and, between rounds of giggling, wobbles over to ralph by the side fence. What with her running nose, teary eyes and upchucking she is really having trouble keeping her insides inside.

Maxine comes out to inform us that in his wife's absence, Goat has served dessert. As Smithy and I follow the others inside I ask him if the dinner with Maxine and Anna is still on the table, as it were.

'Sure is. I think Maxine has already mentioned it to Anna. I've responded on your behalf.'

Maybe I feel a little stupid that I've not yet built up the courage to ask Anna out myself, but to be honest I'm relieved that Maxine has done the hard yards for me.

Seats have again been rearranged and I've done okay – a Naomi sandwich. The Goats are well and truly separated and Maet has Anna's ear, which can only be good for me. Dessert is stupendous even if it wasn't served by Dear, Perfect, Honey, Sweetie or The Wife.

29.

My third weekend in a row paying to live in Glebe while choosing to sleep on the sofa in Bankstown. Last night's fish and chips at the Smithys' meaning more than ever. They and their only son, my brother, continuing to keep me anchored.

Tomorrow we'll venture to Snapper Street, not in a limo like we used to but still grandly enough.

Because of the need to remain straight for tonight's dinner with Anna and Maxine, Smithy and I watch the *Jerry Springer* tapes without the benefit of drugs. Of course, Smithy is able to offer further insights anyhow, given his recent book. Maxine has chosen the restaurant, near her place at Edgecliff. We'll take the train and whack the no doubt hefty bill on Jeff's credit card.

'So how do you feel about Maxine?' I ask Smithy as we wander a great maze of townhouses, looking for the one named twenty-nine.

'She's okay; her hair's a bit much, probably a little serious for me. Could be because she's older but she told me the other night that she's sick of being number three or eight in other people's lives – all her friends and family have partners and kids, bigger priorities. Says she wants to be someone's number one, full member not just an associate – guess that's where Sebastian comes in. She might just see me as a dog replacement.'

Smithy continues to amaze me – is he learning all this from *Jerry Springer* and the net? 'You're much bigger than a Maltese terrier,' I observe. 'You also smoke way more dope than one.'

Smithy grins. 'They tend to drink a fuckin' lot though.'

Holding back her ferocious fur ball Maxine lets us in and suggests we make ourselves comfortable in her living room while she finishes getting ready. Anna hasn't arrived yet. The house is stylish and small, not unlike Maxine herself if it weren't for her tall hair. I head straight for the bookcase and Smithy checks out her DVDs. A surveillance camera would have him for a thief and me a nerd.

Browsing her shelves I start to wonder what varied and bizarre interests Maxine has. Titles such as *Economic Rationalism and the Politics of Self*, *Lesbian Modelling in the Post-Feminist Era* and *The Anthropology of Ancient Death Masks* make me start to dread post-dinner conversation, what with Smithy and I keen to wax on about *Seinfeld* or our favourite fast foods. With relief I note that nearly all the books bear the same esoteric publisher's logo and decide that Maxine must have worked at that house before K&D, the books probably chosen by colour and size, to fit the décor, rather than for their dry content.

For a moment I wonder if Anna has backed out – even though she probably thinks it's just four friends and not a double-date, and she's probably right. As I turn to voice my concern to Smithy she knocks on the door just as Maxine re-appears smelling expensive. Anna looks fantastic, her hair enjoying the obvious benefits of regular, liberal shampooing. She kisses each of us on the cheek and the thought that the swoon I feel might appear as any of a range of contradictory emotions is enough to have me search out a mirror so I can see what my face is doing. My tongue must be hanging out, Sebastian style, as Smithy whispers to me to think about Margaret Thatcher.

The five-minute walk to the restaurant has Maxine panting for the cigarettes she's given up. For the briefest of whiles she walks ahead with Smithy, pre-sumably for a passive smoke, so I take the opportunity to offer Anna condolences on her recent break-up.

'No matter – it really wasn't working. I can see that now.'

'So single again, huh?' I venture.

'Not for too long, I hope.'

'Anyone in mind?' Sometimes I wish I could just shut-up.

'Yes,' Anna says, but adds no more.

Already. Fuck it.

Formulaic pale floorboards, thin, black-attired waiters and chrome furniture greet us as we are escorted to the only remaining table by Leonardo DiCaprio's better-looking brother. It takes DiCaprio nearly half an hour to venture back with water, but he's forgotten the menus. This is fine by me as Anna is having a great time chatting about any topic we swing her way, but Maxine is agitated by the lack of attention from the waiter. Either she's embarrassed because the restaurant was her choice, or she's gagging for a fag.

We are allowed to sip on water without the intrusion of menus for another fifteen minutes, until Maxine whips out her mobile, calls the restaurant, and asks the maitre d', only ten metres away, to 'Please send a waiter over to the table by the front window – the one with the four starving people.'

When DiCaprio does arrive with menus Maxine grabs his wrist and holds him while we scan the bill of fare so she can give him our entrees and mains before he disappears. Nearly every option on the menu has at least five competing flavours so that each selection is guaranteed to include at least one ingredient you have no fucking idea what it is. But for Maxine's sake we move quickly, and Smithy and I stick together ordering the least bizarre combinations we can find. Maxine hasn't completely lost her sense of humour. She recalls a quote she read in some email: *A person who is nice to you, but rude to the waiter, is not a nice person.* This compels Smithy to set one of his infamous challenges. 'If the first lot of food doesn't arrive before someone comes along and unleashes that dog tied to the street sign we are out of here.'

Maxine accepts the deal on behalf of the rest of us, and ups the ante. 'If we do leave then I'm driving us all to one of Smithy's locals, in Bankstown.'

'But that's nearly an hour away. We'll be starving,' I say. How could we find anywhere in Bankstown that Anna and Maxine will feel comfortable in?

Maxine responds. 'That's the deal – we'd probably be onto dessert in a cheap and cheerful before we get served with an entree in any of the places around here.'

Just at that moment the dog takes a walk and so do we.

'It's a choice between Get It India and Happy Sun Chinese,' Smithy says as Maxine stops directly outside the strip of cheap restaurants that run along the railway line.

'I'm just ecstatic at being able to park right outside my destination. Like they do on television,'
Maxine declares.

'I choose Chinese,' Anna says. She's also having
a ball.

'Just beware,' I say. 'It's the sort of Chinese that
has garlic bread on the menu. But I'll concede the
food is nearly restaurant quality.'

Smithy nods his head in agreement as Anna and
Maxine laugh.

We make our way into the Chinese after Smithy
sticks his head inside the mini-mart to say 'G'day
Apu' to the cheery Indian guy who has sold the same
dusty products from this spot for as long as anyone
can remember. Unbeknown to me, but not Smithy,
one of the barmen from The Oasis, Stan, is moon-
lighting as a waiter in the Happy Sun. Stan makes
a fuss of welcoming us and, much to Maxine's joy,
we have menus and an attentive waiter, pad in hand,
within a minute. The most expensive item on the
menu, Peking Duck or as Jeff thought it was called,
Peeking Duck – is cheaper than all of the mains at
our last stop. Most other dishes here are cheaper than
the beers there.

Our friendly waiter does a great job of taking
our order, completely ignoring us when we order something that he doesn't recommend and only recording
dishes that he'd be happy to see us consume. His new

boss keeps a stern eye on him so he is unable verbally to steer us away from the dodgy stuff that he's no doubt been encouraged to push. We just have to keep nominating dishes until we strike the ones that he'll write down for us.

'If so much of the stuff here is questionable why did you suggest this place?' Anna whispers to Smithy.

'Well, at least here we have a guide, directing the way through the crap. You won't get that at places that don't know you.'

Anna nods in agreement.

After a successfully quick meal Maxine suggests that we have coffee back at our place, Smithy's place. I can tell that Maya has been over this evening as Coke cans teeter by the bin in the kitchen. She's also left some photos on Jeff's sofa, my weekend bed. They're from before the accident, the day we went to the beach, Jeff excited about his upcoming interview, me hearing about the job that I had no idea would be mine. As we've spent half the time at the Chinese restaurant talking about him, Anna and Maxine are keen to look at the photos of Jeff. While Smithy is making instant coffee in the kitchen Anna grabs one of the photos with Jeff and Maya in it and asks if she can borrow it. I ask why but she just gives me a smile and touches my hand. 'Sure,' I say. 'Of course.'

30.

'She gave you her number – you know what that's for don't you?' Smithy says. 'To fuckin' call her on!'

'What about Maxine?' I attempt to deflect his thrust. 'She wanted to stay last night.'

I've never known Smithy to pass on a certain shag before but I certainly appreciated it. If he screwed Maxine, then in time, when she was still keen and he'd moved on, my job would likely be screwed as well. Hope she didn't waste a bath bomb on him.

'She had to give Anna a lift home.' Smithy attempts to cover up his good deed. 'Anyway we are talking about you and a chick you actually like – ring and invite her to the Snapper Street barbeque.'

'Are you mad?'

'If you two are going to become an item she has to see you in your natural environment. Anyway, she had a good time last night didn't she?'

'I guess so.'

Surprisingly, she did enjoy herself in my world. Fuck it, I decide, and grab the phone.

'Hi Anna, its Declan McPherson. You're probably busy but I was wondering if you wanted to come to a family barbeque at Hurstville today with me and Smithy?'

One Mississippi, two Mississippi . . .

'That'd be great, when and where?'

'Oh, um, do you want us to collect you or . . .'

'No, it's out of the way. Just give me the address and I'll meet you there.'

'It's two Snapper Street, Hurstville. No need to bring anything. Smithy and I are catching a ride with his parents – we'll definitely be there by twelve.'

'That's fine – see you then.'

Smithy chucks me a fresh bottle of shampoo.

Thankfully Smithy has the presence of mind to roll a spliff for the walk to his parents' place. The soft puffs of flat-bottomed clouds adrift on the pale blue sky hanging above us look just like those in the opening credits of *The Simpsons*. After stepping around old Silk's paw-prints in the path out front of his grandmother's house Smithy goes in to collect Maisie while I wait outside worrying how Anna will fit in with today's motley crew. What will she baulk at most: the oldies who whisper when they mention the word 'Asians'? Great Aunt Gaye's chihuahua with the uncanny resemblance to Bette Davis? Or maybe the neighbour's slightly retarded grandson Jake, who'll welcome Anna with an interrogation of what her favourite things are then spend the rest of the day screaming out the names of airlines as planes pass so far overhead that unless he has the eyesight of an owl he couldn't hope to be accurate.

As we all fall out of Mr Smithy's unlimo-like car, dragging Sylvia with us, I realise it's good Anna didn't take up my offer of a lift. But then to my horror I see that Anna is already in the vast backyard, being interviewed by Jake as a game of cricket grinds on around them.

'Favourite animal?'

'Duck.'

'Favourite milk flavour?'

'Chocolate.'

'Favourite fruit flavour?'

'Lime.'

'Favourite . . .'

I'm impressed by the speed of Anna's responses but interrupt as quickly as I can. Jake has been distracted anyway, looking up in the sky at a mechanical insect and screaming at the top of his lungs 'Singapore!'

I assure Anna that the day is not over yet. She protests that there is no need for an apology, and I take her to meet Mr and Mrs Smithy.

It's all smiles as Anna charms them immediately while I note scattered tumbleweeds of soft pink cotton in her freshly washed hair and hope beyond reason that Anna launched a new towel this morning on my account. Smithy's mum gives me an embarrassing thumbs-up while Anna is still looking so I turn on my heels and introduce Anna to Lester as he prepares the barbeque for his first batch of sausages.

'You're not a vegetarian are you, Anna?' Mrs Smithy asks.

Les pre-empts. 'We've got chicken as well.'

'It's okay, I'm not a vegetarian,' Anna says smiling.

In desperate need for a grandchild of her own Mrs Smithy follows Anna and me to a table already loaded with cold food and some fries for the kids. A herbal-looking woman who I've seen at the last five of these barbeques is blowing on the hot chips before passing them to her toddler son. The toddler's elder sister is also hoeing into the chips and when Gaye comes along to re-load the bowl the girl announces, 'Fucking excellent chips Gaye!'

Anna catches her breath, but Gaye barely blinks. By way of explanation the herbal mother turns to us and proudly says, 'Breeze has been taught that using such words in a positive context is fine.'

Mrs Smithy tells Anna that I used to be a precocious child as well. 'Dec loved to read!'

Anna turns to Mrs Smithy as if I'm not there.

'Bev, I notice you only ever call Declan Dec. Smithy does as well, so do you think he'd mind if I did too?'

I jump in, embarrassed. 'No worries.'

'Emirates!' Jake shouts.

'Fucking top shot!' Breeze yells, watching as her father belts the ball into a neighbour's yard.

Gorging ourselves on the initial round of sausages we watch Smithy overshadow everybody at cricket and laugh when the herbal mother absentmindedly blows on a chip before passing it to her husband, now fielding as close to the food table as possible. The minute Mrs Smithy leaves, Anna leans over and kisses me softly on the lips. I brush the side of her face with the back of my hand and place a light kiss on her lower lip, remembering to resist going the tongue.

'What brought that on?' I ask, gob-smacked. Then, in retreat. 'I mean it was great, I just didn't think you liked me.'

'I've only just met you Dec. I knew Declan the work guy but now I've met Dec and I like him. A lot.'

Having, for the first time that I can recall, outlasted the cricket match we thank Gaye and Les for another year before checking that we've said good-bye to the few others that remain in the now unlit backyard. Anna kindly offers to give me and Smithy a lift back and I suggest she might like to hang out a while at my place, my place in Bankstown.

And out of the darkness a cry of 'United!'

31.

'Was that Ash from the *Daily Tele*?' I ask Maet who
has spent the last hour whispering into his phone.

'Yeah, how did you know?' Maet replies coolly
through the flimsy partition that is meant to allow
such calls to be private.

'I've been trying to contact him myself all morning
about geeing up a piece on the author of *Mango
Days* before she arrives.'

'Leave it till tomorrow Dec – he's pretty busy,'
Maet says suspiciously.

As Ashley, the Features Editor from the *Daily
Telegraph* is one of Maet's best contacts I decide not
to push it, although as far as I know Maet isn't touring
anyone for a while. He's till basking in the light of
Smithy's recent media blitz.

After briefly focusing on work, I allow my mind
to once more settle in with Anna – my brain's equiva-
lent of a screen saver. Since the barbeque at Snapper
Street the good moments have become so plentiful
that nominations for most significant Anna moment

have become too numerous to remember. My smile is stuck and my hair shines.

My mind's free-wheeling is interrupted by Naomi on Reception, the new, confident, post-trivia-night Naomi on Reception.

'Ash from the *Tele* on three, returning your calls.'

'Hey Ash, thanks for getting back to me.'

'No worries, what you got happening?'

'Got a US author coming out next month and just thought you might be able to squeeze in a profile piece while she's here. I'll send you a copy of the final book soon. Anyway, Maet tells me you're flat out with his gig so we can chat about it later if you like.'

'Cool, by the way I've sent Maet the copy for the "class divide" piece and I need his okay before my meeting with Wakeham this afternoon. Do you know where Maet is? He hasn't got back to me.'

I've got no idea what he's talking about, but my curiosity is aroused by his reference to the city's mayor, Ross Wakeham. 'Email me the article,' I say, 'and I'll run it down to Maet. He's at lunch downstairs.'

Almost immediately I've got mail, but it takes me a while to get my head around what appears to be a scathing editorial about the city's programme of erecting park benches dedicated to high-profile Sydney-siders who've carked it.

I print out the email and tell Naomi on Reception that I'll be out for a few minutes but she's too preoccupied with her latest boyfriend, one of the new young guys from editorial, the Asian-looking one, to bother registering my departure.

Ironically, I find Maet drinking his lunch, a banana smoothie, atop a fresh park bench that I can't recall having seen outside Universal Tower before today. This one, made like the others that are springing up daily from real sandstone and sturdy strips of teak, is dedicated to the memory of a recently deceased ex-Rugby Union star.

Maet slides over so I can join him and checks the draft article carefully as I sit in silence wondering what this is all about.

Eventually Maet seems satisfied with the piece. He hands the copy back with a knowing grin. 'Did you read this, Dec?' He knows full well that I have.

'Yep. Why is Ash running an editorial past you before it appears?'

'It's not for publication. Ash told me last week that he had an interview with the mayor today so I asked a small favour – a bogus article that Wakeham might like to pre-empt.'

'Huh?'

'These benches have been allocated to a certain section of the community, not to regular people. If Ross Wakeham thinks that Sydney's biggest paper is about to run a piece bagging the fact that only the rich and famous are being included in the program, then what's the bet he'll come up with the idea of reserving a few for less obvious candidates?'

'Not bad,' I say, dawn breaking, 'But what's your involvement?'

'I've given Ash the name of someone he can propose when the Mayor tries to come up with a deceased representative of the unassuming masses, a group he's not overly familiar with.'

'Jeff.'

'Jeff.'

'Hugest scam ever, Maet. I applaud my new hero. But what about the money – don't they cost ten grand each?'

'I'm sure the city will decide to cover the cost when Ash informs the Mayor that Jeff's naive but true-blue battler mates have so far raised $237.80 toward a bench they'd normally have no chance of being awarded.'

'Two hundred dollars? Where did you get that from? I could get more cash than that of off Jeff's credit card alone. Smithy might also relent and ask Jeff's parents for some of the compensation money they got from the dodgy scaffolding company.'

'No Dec, its better this way – a totally paltry-sounding sum will really pull the heart strings of our civic leader.'

'Fuck, you certainly are a senior publicist!'

'If it comes off, consider it a thank-you for what

you guys have done for me,' Maet says. 'You're my friend after all.'

Weird. This person who seems to have it all feels indebted to me and Smithy, who've made a life out of having nothing.

32.

'Can you put Jeffrey in the car please?' Maya calls to Smithy from the kitchen where she's cramming food into a hamper already bulging with baby paraphernalia.

Maet and I roll another round of spliffs so in total we'll have ten, varying in thickness. The cones I've had for breakfast have me fumbling the joints into my pocket as Smithy carries Jeffrey over, pointing to Maet and me in turn. With a massive smile, he re-introduces us to Maya's newborn boy: 'This is Fruit and this is Vegetable.'

Maet laughs and I knock my head on the makeshift coffee table as I attempt to scoop up scattered spliffs.

Rat-Boy missed his mother's cooking more than he enjoyed Smithy's company, so Maya arrived with her baby directly from the hospital, moving into my old room and filling any voids left by Jeff and then me. The thought of them all here together while I'm in Glebe has got me yearning for a coil in my back and a half-eaten yeeros under my pillow. The sofa so has my name on it that I could read it from space.

We pack ourselves into Maet's car. Maya, who is breastfeeding, can remain our chauffeur for some months yet. Smithy and I sit either side of the baby capsule. As I watch my best mate triple-check the capsule's seat belt I notice redness around his throat.

'What's with your neck? Have you been wearing a tie? Have you been to a job interview?' – the questions forming in time with my gradually clearing mind.

Smithy peers at the sleeping baby, whose long Jeff eyelashes rest upon tiny cheekbones. 'Young Jeffrey, please note Vegetable has changed his name back to Sherlock.'

Saving the spliffs until we've arrived at The Domain for our first family picnic at Jeff's bench we decide to entertain Jeffrey instead, managing to make as many ga-ga sounds as we do when we're totally stoned.

'Jeffrey, that's where Dex lives, for now.' Smithy points to a street sign warning of Glebe's proximity. And as we cruise through the city Smithy points out to Jeffrey where Declan works.

Maet, Smithy and I haul all the stuff that is required by one so small as Maya strides across the grass, her legs speeding up as if they're trying to get away from her body. It seems fitting that her first visit to Jeff's new sofa comes under a benevolent blue sky. The sun shines as strongly on Jeff's plaque as it does on those that celebrate the lives of the famous and publicly acclaimed.

Jeff Acton. Friend.

Maya starts to unpack the food directly in front of the pristine park bench that is firmly cemented to the earth's skin, never to be shed. I look around for Anna and spot her making her way over to us with another basket of food. The lawn is so broad that we're able to polish off the first couple of joints by the time Anna reaches us. She is meeting Maya for the first time, but my concern that they might not get on dissipates immediately when Anna pulls out of her hamper a finished copy of *Mango Days*, the jacket featuring a photograph of Jeff and Maya sucking on a couple of fat mangoes in the front of Smithy's old car.

Smithy holds up the baby, introducing him to Anna and this time to me, Dec.

I look at Anna in amazement as she takes a seat on Jeff's bench, sliding to one end so that the rest of us can all squeeze on as well. Maya sits in the middle of the bench, her back warmed by Jeff's plaque, holding the baby who sleeps again. Lined up we watch the afternoon pass as if we are all sat on Jeff's bed watching a movie on television, smoking spliffs, together.

Wakefield Press is an independent publishing and
distribution company based in Adelaide, South Australia.
We love good stories and publish beautiful books.
To see our full range of titles, please visit our website at
www.wakefieldpress.com.au.

Wakefield Press thanks Fox Creek Wines
and Arts South Australia for their support.